"Do I understand?" Kate said at last

She took a moment to swallow her fury. "Oh, yes, Mr. Sarsby, I understand, all right. You think no one is interested in anyone but you—you think we're all watching with bated breath to see what wonderful thing you'll do next."

Her voice shook a little despite all her efforts. "All right, I admit you've shown enormous determination and courage—but it doesn't mean you can expect admiration for the rest of your life. You have to earn that too, Mr. Sarsby. And you won't earn it by being insufferably arrogant."

Max sat back, looking a little stunned. Then his hand covered Kate's, large and warm.

"Let's start again, shall we?" he said softly, an intentness in his smoldering blue gaze. "Let's go right back to the beginning and start again."

Nicola West, born on the south coast of England, now lives in central England with her husband and family. She always knew she wanted to write. She started writing articles on many subjects, a regular column in a county magazine, children's stories and women's magazine stories before tackling her first book. Though she had three novels published before she became a Harlequin author, she feels her first novel for Harlequin was a turning point in her career. Her settings are usually places that she has seen for herself.

Books by Nicola West

HARLEQUIN ROMANCE

HARLEQUIN PRESENTS

SNOW DEMON

Nicola West

Harlequin Books

TORONTO • NEW YORK • LONDON
AMSTERDAM • PARIS • SYDNEY • HAMBURG
STOCKHOLM • ATHENS • TOKYO • MILAN

Original hardcover edition published in 1989
by Mills & Boon Limited

ISBN 0-373-03089-4

Harlequin Romance first edition November 1990

CHAPTER ONE

'H<small>I</small>.' Kate Markham dropped her flight-bag on the seat next to the tall, black-haired man already seated, and gave him a cheerful grin. 'I think this is my seat. Mind if I stretch over you while I squash my jacket into the locker?'

The man gave her a non-committal shrug. Feeling slightly irritated, Kate pushed her thick ski-jacket into the confined space and sat down beside him, slightly breathless. She pushed back her long honey-blonde hair.

'Looks as if we'll be taking off on time,' she remarked chattily. Flying always made her want to talk—to take her mind off that great space of air between her and the ground, she guessed. 'I'm glad of that—I hate the hanging around you so often get at airports these days, don't you? Are you going on holiday?'

He put down his newspaper with a barely concealed sigh. 'I suppose you'd probably call it that. I'm going skiing.'

'Really?' Kate said in surprise. 'But it's early for package holidays—ours don't start until next week.'

'Ours?'

'I'm a rep with Stanton Holidays,' Kate explained. 'I've already been in Austria for a fortnight, actually, getting everything set up—I just had to slip back to London for a few days to finalise things at that end—and now I'm going to get ready for the first arrivals. Which company are you going with? I didn't know any of them were starting before us.'

'I don't go with a package company,' he said frostily. 'I'm going privately. I don't much care for humanity *en masse*—especially on the ski-slopes.'

Get you! Kate thought. But she'd been well-trained not to reveal her feelings, and all she said was, 'Well, I hope you've chosen somewhere quiet to do your skiing, then. It's been getting more and more popular as a holiday. Nearly thirty per cent more people have already booked for this year with my company, and——'

'Spare me the gory details,' he begged, opening his paper again. 'I just hope they aren't all going where I'm going. And don't ask me where that is—as far as I'm concerned, the less people who know about it, the better. Especially as I intend to stay for the whole winter.'

'The whole winter?' Kate's green eyes widened. 'However can you manage that? Are you a professional?' She looked at him properly for the first time. Surely there was something familiar about that black hair, the straight brows and those strange blue eyes, dark as navy yet overlaid with the brilliance of turquoise? Good-looking enough to be a film or TV star, though she couldn't recall ever having seen him in a film. Yet surely she had, at some time, seen those brilliant eyes looking out of a screen. . .? A faint memory stirred, but refused to define itself more clearly. 'Should I know you?' she asked doubtfully.

The man beside her gave her a glance that was almost contemptuous. 'I doubt it. Your skiing is mostly concerned with package holidays and beginners, I imagine. And I prefer to keep my own company, if you don't mind—on aeroplanes as well as on the ski-slopes.' He shook his paper out, and Kate, infuriated, turned her head away and stared determinedly across the aisle. So he didn't want to make conversation! Fair enough—she wouldn't address one single word more to him during the entire flight. Who cared who he was or what he was doing, anyway?

It was just her bad luck that the seat on her other side should be taken by an elderly lady, whose conversation centred solely around the grandchildren she was going to spend Christmas with in Germany, where her daughter's husband worked. But at least the old woman was friendly. And while her voice meandered on, Kate was free to follow her own train of thought and wonder, yet again, whether it had really been wise to come out to Austria again, so soon after the accident that had made her swear never to go near another ski-slope for the rest of her life.

'Resign?' her boss, Frank Dawson, had exclaimed when she'd first gone to see him a few weeks ago. 'Kate, we can't lose you! You're the best rep we have. Your experience, your personality—everything about you is right. You can't mean it.'

'I do mean it.' Kate sat miserably in front of his desk, the long white envelope containing her formal resignation lying between them. 'You know what happened. I can't face it again—the snow, the skiing. Everyone laughing and happy—not knowing what can happen, how cruel the mountains can be. I don't think I'll ever put on a pair of skis again, Frank. It's over.'

He leaned forwards. 'That's exactly it. It's *over*, Kate. In the past. You've got to put it behind you and go on. It's like falling off a bike—you've got to pick yourself up and get right back in the saddle. It's the only way.'

Kate shook her head, feeling the tears hot in her eyes.

'What happened to me was rather worse than falling off a bike, Frank. Two——'

'I know,' he cut in gently. 'But it still applies. Kate, I'm telling you—if you don't go back to Austria this season, you'll never go back. There'll be a whole, enormous part of your life that you'll never be able to come to terms with. You can't spend the rest of your life running away from memories, Kate. You've got to turn and face them some time—and, believe me, it'll be a lot less painful if you do it now.'

'I can't ski again——she began, but again he broke in.

'Nobody's asking you to ski, Kate. Just go there. Do your job in a place where other people are skiing. Advise them on how to choose their boots, their skis; help them with their problems. And watch them enjoy themselves. That's the best therapy for you, Kate. Maybe you never will ski again—maybe after a while you'll feel able to. But at least you'll have given it a go. You'll have refused to be beaten.' He got up and came to stand behind her, his hand on her shoulder. 'You're not the type to be beaten. If you run away now, and go off to Greece or some other winter holiday spot, you'll be denying your own nature. And that's bad.'

Kate sat silently for a while, feeling the warmth of his hand flow into her body. Frank had always been good to her, right from that first gruelling interview when she had applied for a job as a holiday rep. He'd seen her through the intensive training she and the other reps had undergone—the psychology course, the role-playing, the language examinations. And he'd always been there, at the other end of a telephone, when she'd encountered any serious problems in whatever resort she was working in.

'Don't answer this now, Kate,' he said at last. 'Give it some thought. But there's a special job available—setting up a new resort in a tiny village called St Joachim—and we want you to do it. It'll be a real challenge.' He came round his desk again, and she saw the light of excitement in his heavy face. 'A small place, but there are plenty of nice hotels there, and good nursery slopes. None of the big operators have got in there yet—Stanton Holidays are going to be the first. You'd have to go out pretty soon and see all the hotels—they've been chosen, of course, they're all in the brochure and pretty well booked-up, but the final details would have to be settled on the spot. You'd have to make contact with the ski-school, too, and the ski-hire shop. The groundwork's been done, but the success depends almost entirely on the rep who starts the season. We'd very much like it to be you, Kate.' He paused. 'As I said, don't decide straight away. . .' He reached across and fingered the white envelope. 'I'll keep this for a while, shall I? Until you've finally made up your mind? And then perhaps you'll give me the pleasure of tearing it up.'

Kate lifted her head and looked steadily at him. The fear of the slopes was still with her, but she knew Frank was right. It had to be faced and beaten. And that meant going out to Austria again. Doing the job she was good at.

'You can tear it up now, Frank,' she said quietly. 'I'll take your challenge. And—thanks for bothering.'

His big face split into a broad grin. He came round the desk and put both hands on her shoulders, squeezing them almost painfully in his delight. If he hadn't been English, Kate thought with some amusement, he might have hugged her!

'Kate, that's marvellous!' he declared. 'I can't tell you how pleased I am. And before you change your mind——' He ripped the envelope in half and flung the pieces into the waste-paper basket. 'There! There's no going back now, eh? No going back at all.'

No going back, Kate thought as she sat on the plane and listened to the droning voice beside her. And she felt a tremor somewhere deep inside her body.

It might have helped if she had been able to talk to the man beside her. More and more, she had sought the company of people who knew nothing of her personal tragedy, finding their conversation calming because it was unforced. And he was a skier, too.

But he had made it clear that he didn't want to talk. And, sitting so close to him, Kate had the impression that he was as tense as she was. That there was some deeper reason than mere unsociability for his unfriendly attitude.

Well, if that was so, she would be better to steer clear of him. Just now, she needed someone else's hang-ups about as much as she needed a wooden head. Her own were more than enough to cope with. It was probably just as well that they wouldn't be meeting again once the plane had touched down in Salzburg.

'And this will be your room. You will find it comfortable, I hope.'

Kate stepped inside and looked around. The room was bigger than she'd expected, with the traditional wood-panelled walls and sloping ceiling of an upstairs room in an Austrian farmhouse. There was a comfortable-looking bed covered with a billowing duvet, an easy chair, and a small table with a wooden chair drawn up underneath it where she could do her paperwork. The window led out to a small balcony, and as she crossed the room to look at the view she felt a quickening of her earlier excitement.

'It looks straight out on to the slopes!' Kate exclaimed in German. She watched as a confetti of colourful skiers swooped down the white hill, criss-crossing each other's tracks, marking the freshly fallen snow with the long, evenly spaced loops of expert *wedelning*. For a moment, she felt the urge to get out there with them, refreshing the skill in which she'd taken such joy; then memory flooded back and she turned quickly away.

'Only the nursery slopes, I'm afraid,' Frau Brunner said apologetically. 'Those are the ski instructors—they always practise at this time. The real skiing is up on the mountain, and you must go there by bus. But you know all this already, of course.'

'Yes, I found all those points out when I was here a week or so ago.' Kate smiled at the dumpy little Austrian with her creased, leathery face and smiling eyes. 'The room's lovely, Frau Brunner. I know I'll be very comfortable here.'

The eyes rested on her in frank curiosity. 'You speak very good German, *fräulein*. I would hardly believe you are English.'

Kate laughed. 'That's because I grew up in the Swiss Oberland. My parents lived there most of the year, when my father wasn't abroad on tour. He's a musician.'

'*Ach*, I understand. And they live there still?'

'No, not now. They've gone back to England—my father's not very strong, and he's semi-retired.' She began to unfasten her suitcase. 'I'll unpack now, shall I? I believe you're providing me with an evening meal? Although I expect to eat in the hotel most nights, with the guests—it gives me a chance to get to know them, and they can talk over any problems they might have, too.'

'Yes, you will eat here whenever you wish—as long as you don't mind eating with us.' Frau Brunner's eyes were kind as she looked at the young English girl. 'Supper will be ready in half an hour. Now, you know where everything is—the bathroom, the kitchen. Please tell me if there is anything more you need.'

'I'm sure you've thought of everything.' Kate smiled at her hostess. 'I'll be down in half an hour.'

Frau Brunner closed the door, leaving her alone, and she sat down for a moment on the bed and closed her eyes. Well, that was the first hurdle over. Frau Brunner had asked no questions. And the room was lovely— much better than Kate had expected. Travel companies often expected their couriers to cope in quite cramped accommodation. What was more, there didn't appear to be anyone else staying at the Brunners' farmhouse. Kate found that she had to be quite gregarious enough in the job that she did. The little privacy she could snatch in her own accommodation was extremely valuable to her.

She began again to unpack her suitcase, feeling more light-hearted than she had done for weeks. Pausing for a moment, she went once again to the window and stared out at the brilliant figures swooping down the gleaming white slopes. Tentatively, she allowed her imagination to take her up there with them, feeling herself at the top of the slope with a pair of sharply edged skis under her feet, savouring that last moment before she began her exhilarating descent.

Her cure might indeed be here. Perhaps she might even be able to ski again. And—even more than that— perhaps she could begin at last to forget that other pain: the pain that was David.

She knew there would be little time to wonder whether she had been wise or not.

Being a holiday courier, as she already knew, was hard work, and she would be flung straight into it on her first day in the village. It was already white with snow— auguring a good season, she thought hopefully as she unpacked. Snow was what everyone came for on these holidays, and to arrive complete with skis and find bare earth and rocks was a disappointment even the most experienced courier could not allay. But this village was high enough to expect snow both early and late, and Kate did not anticipate any problems in that direction.

She checked that she had all her papers, including her list of hotels and *Gasthäuser* which Stanton Holidays were using this year. She had, of course, contacted them all on her previous visit, but it was important to see them again. She must develop a good relationship with all those who would be receiving her guests, as well as with the ski-school and the hire shop where many of the holiday-makers would be obtaining their skiing equipment. She also needed to make sure that the accommodation offered was up to standard, and that the guests would be comfortable and happy there.

'Dealing with people is the most important part of the job,' she had been told at her interview, when she'd first applied to work as a courier. 'Do you think you'll be up to it?'

'Can you cope with drunks?' someone else had asked before she could reply, and in seconds all six interviewers had been firing questions at her.

'Accidents? Suppose someone gets badly injured?'

'What would you do if one of your guests simply failed to turn up? Disappeared?'

'What if an elderly passenger has a heart attack during transfer?'

'How would you cope with the persistent complainer?'

'How do you manage if there's a long flight delay. . .the coach doesn't turn up. . .one of the male passengers persists in making advances towards you? Or to one of the lady guests? What if there's a theft? What do you do about missing luggage?'

The interview had gone on and on, with all the possible contingencies covered, and had proved to be only the first step of a training so rigorous that afterwards Kate had felt that anyone who could survive this could survive anything. But suddenly it was all over, and the newly fledged couriers had dispersed to their various destinations, where there was no more play-acting and it was all 'for real', with guests who would be justifiably annoyed if things went wrong, and hoteliers who had their own ideas about how to run their own businesses, and where nothing ever went quite by the book.

It had taught Kate a great deal of self-reliance. And it was to prove to herself that she could cope with anything that life hurled at her that she had come to Austria.

* * *

After a quick bath, Kate slipped into a bright plaid skirt in honour of her first evening at the Brunners', pulled a blue sweater over her head, and gave her long, shining hair a hasty brush before going downstairs to join the Brunner family.

They welcomed her into the big, comfortable kitchen which evidently served as their main living-room, too. The tiled stove gave off a steady warmth, and the wood-panelled walls and bright rugs imparted a cheerful cosiness. The air was filled with the spicy smell of *gulaschsuppe*, and the big table was laid with places for four—Herr and Frau Brunner, their seventeen-year-old son Dieter, who grinned shyly at Kate from his chair, and Kate herself.

'So. You are ready to eat, I think.' Frau Brunner drew her to the table and began to serve the thick, meaty soup into large bowls. 'A long journey always makes one hungry. And the cold weather, too—colder than you have in England, *nicht wahr*?'

Kate began to answer her, but her voice was drowned by a sudden thunderous knocking on the outer door. The four of them paused, spoons half-way to their mouths.

'I will go to see,' Frau Brunner said, getting up. The other three continued with their meal, listening to the voices outside. There was something familiar in the tones of the newcomer, Kate thought, and just as she had realised who it was Frau Brunner came back into the kitchen, preceding a tall, black-haired man with angry blue eyes and a grim mouth. Kate lowered her spoon slowly into her bowl. What he was angry about, she had no idea, but anyone could see that it was directed at her.

'So it's you I've got to thank for having nowhere to stay!' he greeted her without preamble.

Kate blinked. 'I beg your pardon?'

'He says he has business with you,' Frau Brunner intervened anxiously, her English clearly not good enough to follow their conversation. 'But if you wish him to leave——'

'No, it's all right, Frau Brunner,' Kate said quickly. 'Though I don't see why he should come bursting into your kitchen in this way.' She turned back, wondering why it was that his presence seemed to fill the room. 'Don't you think you're being rather rude, marching in here?' she demanded. 'This is a private home. If you must see me—though I can't think why you should— you could at least have the courtesy of acknowledging the owners. And you could perhaps wait until we've finished our meal.'

'I'm sorry, I didn't know you'd be eating.' The apology was too cursory to be genuine, but when he turned to the Brunners and apologised again—in impeccable German, this time—his tone was unexpectedly sincere. 'I apologise, *mein Herr*, for interrupting your meal. I simply wish to speak with Miss Markham over a matter of accommodation. If we might perhaps use another room——'

'Accommodation?' Kate broke in. 'But your accommodation has nothing to do with me. You're not travelling with Stanton Holidays.'

'Thank heaven,' he said tersely. 'But allow me to correct you—my accommodation, or lack of it, has a great deal to do with you. Do you realise that you and your precious holiday company have taken over the whole of St Joachim? That after Sunday, when the first of your—your *mob* arrive, there won't be a bed to be had in the place?' Apparently forgetting once more that he was in a private house, he flung himself into Frau Brunner's large armchair, close to the stove, and stared moodily at the coloured rug at his feet. 'I've been coming to this village for the past ten years, and it's always been a haven of peace and quiet,' he said bitterly. 'And now you're turning it into a snowy version of Blackpool!'

Kate felt her indignation rise. 'Indeed I'm not! And neither are Stanton Holidays. Look, the village *wants* skiers to come here. They've made a deliberate effort to become a real ski-resort. The hotels have expanded. The ski-school has enlarged; it's taken on English-speaking instructors. They've encouraged Stanton's—and the other operators too, we're not the only one——'

'You're the biggest. And what's more, if I understand it correctly, next week—which should be one of the quietest of the season—the place is going to be alive with *beginners*.'

'Yes, that's quite right,' Kate said stiffly. 'Beginners. Not creatures from under a stone, or things from outer space, as your tone seems to suggest. Perfectly ordinary, decent people who want to learn to ski. Just as I imagine you had to learn, once upon a time.'

'All right, all right,' he said. 'So everyone's got the right to learn. But why *here*? It's always been so unspoilt.'

'A pity we can't say the same about you,' Kate said. 'It strikes me you've had everything your own way up till now. You can't have a whole village to yourself, Mr——' To her annoyance, she realised that she'd never heard his name, though he clearly knew hers. 'Anyway, I don't accept that we've spoilt it,' she added lamely.

'And I don't know what you think I can do about it either. Why come to me?'

'Because it's your gang that have taken over the best hotel in the place, that's why. As well as quite a lot of the others. I've been traipsing round for the past hour, looking for somewhere to stay. And don't tell me I ought to have booked ahead—I've never needed to. Not at this time of year.' He sighed and then shrugged. 'I just thought you might have some idea where there might be a room. I'm all right until Sunday—but after that, I'm out. And I don't fancy unpacking just for a few days— I'd sooner find somewhere that can take me tonight, for the whole winter.'

'The whole winter?' Out of courtesy to the Brunners, their conversation had been conducted in German. Now Dieter Brunner broke in, his eyes alight with excitement. 'Now I know who you are! You're Max Sarsby. The downhill champion. You had that terrible accident a few years ago. But—I thought they said you'd never ski again?'

'They said I'd never walk again,' Max Sarsby said grimly. 'But, as you can see, they were wrong.'

Dieter turned to his mother. His body was almost vibrating with excitement.

'He can have my room, *Mutter*. I can sleep in the small room. Imagine—a ski champion staying here for the whole winter!' He swung back to Max Sarsby, his face glowing. 'Please—I insist! You will be comfortable—ask Miss Markham, here. You are comfortable, Miss Markham, *nicht wahr*? You are happy, well-fed?'

His enthusiasm made Kate laugh, in spite of her dismay at the idea of having Max Sarsby staying in the same house. 'Honestly, Dieter, I've only been here an

hour myself! But yes, I think I will be very comfortable.'
She looked at the soup cooling in her bowl. 'And well-
fed, too.'

'Then it is settled,' Dieter said positively, and looked
at his parents for confirmation. Kate looked at them,
too. They seemed slightly dazed—and who could blame
them?—but, to her surprise, they appeared to be as
eager as their son to have Max Sarsby staying in their
home for the whole of the winter.

'You must be hungry, too,' Frau Brunner declared,
and fetched another bowl. 'Move, Dieter, and make
room for Herr Sarsby. And then you will help me to
arrange the rooms.'

Max Sarsby, looking equally dazed, sat down beside
Kate. She was vibrantly aware of his body, close to
hers—the massiveness of it, the warmth, the potential
power and strength. She stared at her bowl and picked
up her spoon again.

'I must just get one thing straight,' he said as Frau
Brunner placed a steaming bowl of *gulaschsuppe* before
him. 'I never made it to champion. It was on the last
run that I had my accident—and although I was making
the best time at that point, being carried off on a
stretcher does count as a disqualification!' He lifted his
head and stared at the wall. 'I never made it then. But
next time I will. Don't be in any doubt about that.'

The other four people in the room stared at him. Kate
could feel the power in him as he spoke, the utter,
ruthless determination—a determination that would let
nothing stand in its way.

She shivered a little. She had only once before met quite
that quality of determination. And it frightened her.

CHAPTER TWO

IF KATE had comforted herself with the thought that a ski champion and a holiday courier need never meet, the next few days proved her wrong. Busy as she was—finalising the arrangements for her first week's skiers, meeting their flights in Salzburg, collecting her flock together, making sure they were all on the right coach, and finally seeing them all to the correct hotels—she was nevertheless constantly aware of his presence. She saw him in the village, stacking his skis on the back of the bus which ran to the main skiing area; she caught glimpses of him in restaurants, drinking hot chocolate or coffee with the chief ski instructor, whom he seemed to know well. And she was forever meeting him at the Brunners' house, going in and out with skis, sitting at the breakfast-table or at supper, his dark, brilliant eyes meeting hers enigmatically across the wood-panelled room.

Once Dieter had reminded her, she knew that the name and face had been niggling at her memory ever since she'd first seen him on the plane. Not that she had ever been very interested in competition skiing, but nobody at all interested in the sport could avoid hearing some of the top names. Girardelli, Zurbriggen, Schneider—all were names spoken with awe in the mountain cafés and village restaurants where skiers gathered to drink *glühwein* and hot chocolate. And, until a year or two ago, Sarsby had looked liked joining them.

'He really was the tops,' Julie, the Stanton rep based in the next village, told her as they travelled to Salzburg on the empty coach. 'And then, in the last leg of the race, something went wrong. I don't think they ever really knew what happened. He was carried off half-dead, and had to be more or less pinned together again. Broken hip, pelvis, legs, ribs—you name it, he broke it. I mean, it really was horrific. Nobody thought he'd ever walk again, let alone ski.'

Kate covered her eyes for a moment. Only her own unhappiness could have made her forget the glamorous champion, expected to walk away with all the prizes during the great skiing championships, who had instead ended up in a hospital bed, his career apparently at an end. 'Didn't they call him the "Snow Devil", or something?' she asked.

'"Snow Demon",' Julie said. 'Someone used it one day and the next minute they were all saying it. It suited him so well, too. He didn't seem human when he was up there in the snow. He seemed more at home on skis than in shoes. It was a real tragedy when he was hurt.' She leaned over the table, eyes shining. 'To think he's actually *here*—and skiing again. What's he doing, Kate? Does he intend to go in for the championships again? And why doesn't anyone know about it?'

'Because he doesn't want them to, I guess. He told me he likes solitude. And apparently he can't stand anyone who doesn't ski as well as he does himself.'

Julie nodded. 'He had a reputation for being on the arrogant side, I remember. And for ambition, too—he was determined to get to the top, and didn't much care who he trod on to get there. Well, that was what they said—I don't know how true it was. What do you think,

Kate? You're staying in the same house—what's he really like?'

Kate frowned thoughtfully. 'I don't really know. I've hardly seen anything of him. Yes, I'd say he was arrogant—but I've only known him a few days. And if what you say about his accident is true, I can only admire him for coming back and starting again. It takes courage to go back to something that's nearly killed you.'

'Yes, I suppose it does.' Julie rested her chin on her hand, gazing dreamily out of the coach window at the sparkling mountains. 'Well, whatever he's like, I wouldn't mind getting to know him a bit better. You've got to admit, he is ultra-dishy. That black wavy hair—those eyes. And that gorgeous smile!' She shook her head. 'You wouldn't care to swap jobs with me, I suppose?'

Kate laughed. 'No, I wouldn't! And not because of the demon skier, either. Frau Brunner's breakfasts are much too good to pass up, and I'm not sure your particular brand of adoration would be at all good for Max Sarsby—I'd guess that's something his ego *doesn't* need. He's quite pleased enough with himself as it is.'

'All right, Kate, you dog in the manger. Keep him all to yourself,' Julie said good-temperedly. 'But keep me posted—right?'

'There'll be nothing to keep you posted about,' Kate said firmly, gathering her papers together. 'Anyway, we're nearly at the airport now, and it won't be long before we're inundated with beginners. It's a good idea, having these weeks specially for people who've never skied before, but they can be hard work. I don't suppose there'll be any time to worry about Max Sarsby—even if I felt inclined to. And I don't imagine he'll be asking to join any of our evening excursions!'

'Now there's a thought,' Julie said wickedly. 'I wonder if he'd like a trip on a bob-sleigh. I've always fancied myself on the Cresta Run. . . All right, Kate. I'll leave him alone. Though why you should set yourself up as his protector, I don't know—you don't seem to like the man at all! Or could you just be protesting a little too much?'

As the coach came to a halt, Julie stood up and skipped off as soon as the door slid open. Kate followed more slowly. Julie's last words, casual though they'd been, had given her something of a shock.

She'd already been aware that Max Sarsby was an exceptionally attractive man. But had she quite realised the effect he had on her? Had she allowed herself to acknowledge the full impact of his personality, the sheer magnetism that he exercised apparently without effort?

Perhaps her words had given away more of herself than she knew. Perhaps she really had sounded as if she was trying to protect Max—while at the same time conveying an instinctive hostility. And perhaps Julie had seen more deeply into the reasons for her ambivalent attitude.

The truth is, Kate thought in a moment of clear-sightedness, I *am* attracted to the kind of man Max Sarsby is. I do like strength and power, and the kind of personality that's larger than life—that sets out to achieve something and won't rest until it's got there.

Unfortunately, she also knew what effect a man with such a personality could have on those most closely involved with him. And she had made a vow not to get involved with such a man again.

For her, Max Sarsby could be bad news. It was best to avoid him as much as possible. Or else do as Julie had suggested—and swap digs.

Kate smiled. Wasn't she behaving just a little like some hysterical schoolgirl? Max had shown no interest whatsoever in her as a person. He had made it clear that he was interested only in his skiing. And since she had an exacting job of her own to do, their paths need only occasionally cross—even if they were staying in the same house.

The first flight from Gatwick had arrived, bringing the first excited and somewhat apprehensive beginners. Kate hurried forward to meet them.

On the following day, the season began in earnest.

To Kate's relief, it was a sparkling morning. There had been a light snowfall overnight, but the clouds had rolled away, leaving a sky that was bluer and brighter than that of most English summer days. The nursery slopes gleamed, the *pistes* as smooth as an iced cake, and the fir trees bore a fringe of lacy white along each of their branches. The roofs of the buildings were bordered with icicles like a frieze of broken crystal, and the little dome on top of the church tower glowed like a freshly peeled onion ready for the pot.

The beginners were all clustered at the foot of the nursery slopes, staggering awkwardly about in their stiff ski-boots, their skis carried over their shoulders. Kate had impressed upon them that they should not put their skis on until told to do so by an instructor. 'Otherwise they won't know you're a beginner,' she had explained, 'and you'll find yourself up on a black run before you know where you are. Yes, you can laugh—but it has happened! So don't be tempted.'

She moved among them, making sure they were all happy with the equipment they'd hired—beginners rarely had their own boots or skis, preferring to wait to find out if they actually liked the sport before buying expensive equipment. Everyone was in a smart new ski-suit though, either a one-piece or jacket and salopettes, and the colours mingled in a kaleidoscope of brilliance against the gleaming snow.

'Have you all got your vouchers and lift-passes?' Kate asked. 'Right, just wait here and in a few minutes the ski instructors will be with us. Watch that hill. They're going up on the T-bar now, see?'

The crowd of people turned obediently to see the red-clad figures of the ski instructors riding in twos on the T-bar lift that went up the highest of the nursery slopes. Kate knew that to beginners this slope looked frighten-ingly high and steep—yet in two or three days they, too, would be riding that T-bar and coming down the broad white expanse. And by Friday, they would be gathering at the top in a fever of impatience to ski in the weekly race and show just how much they had learned.

She shaded her eyes with one hand and gazed upwards. The instructors had disappeared momentarily at the top, and she imagined them gliding down the first gentle track which led to the sharp edge over which they would soon appear. From there, they would have a view of the whole village and far beyond into the mountains. She thought of skiing those distant peaks, leaving the 'ski circus' of lifts and prepared *pistes* to go alone into deep powder snow, challenging the mountains, becom-ing part of the silent wilderness of snow and ice. That

was what Max Sarsby liked—to get right away from the
humanity that seethed around popular routes, skiing
from the top of one lift to the bottom of another. For a
moment, standing there among the chattering horde, she
felt in complete sympathy with him. She envied him his
solitude and freedom to go where he liked.

'Here they come!'

The cry went up from several voices at once as the red
figures appeared at the top of the escarpment and
seemed to hang there, poised, for a brief moment, before
swooping in graceful curves down the wide slope.
Together, in perfect harmony, they twisted and turned,
now linking arms to ski in formation, now breaking away
to form a line of almost geometric precision, skiing across
each other's tracks to produce the typical loops of
wedelning. The watchers fell silent, aware that they were
being treated to a display of expertise that could only be
gained through years of practice. The instructors—men
and women, all glowing with the tan that never left
them—reached the foot of the slope and skidded to a
halt, smilingly pleased with their own performance, and
the chief instructor glided over to Kate's group.

'All beginners here, please.' Quickly, he sorted them
out into classes of ten and assigned each one to an
instructor. Still carrying their skis, they trooped over to
the gentlest of the nursery slopes and began awkwardly
to get ready. Kate watched for a moment. They were
now in the care of the ski-school, and with luck she
wouldn't see any of them until late afternoon. She turned
her attention to the few people who were left—the
intermediate and advanced skiers who wanted to go into
a ski-school class to improve their technique, and were

waiting to do the test run that would enable the ski instructors to grade them into suitable classes.

'Always a bit nerve-racking, this part,' remarked a man standing close to her. He was one of her guests, but she had had little chance to speak to him yet, since he had brought his own skis and boots and seemed able to find his own way about without the assistance of a rep. 'I'm always slightly afraid I'll ski unusually well and get put into a class that's too advanced for me. I don't think I'm ready for mogul-bashing yet.'

Kate laughed. 'I think the instructors are pretty good judges. They won't take you up on the black runs straight away. Anyway, they want you over at the lifts now, so good luck.'

The man grinned cheerfully at her and slid away to the queue that was already forming at the T-bar. Kate stood watching for a moment, then turned away. There was just time to grab a quick coffee before she had to go to the little information office and telex her report to London.

'Not taking the chance of a quick run or two?'

Kate jumped a little and turned swiftly. There was no mistaking that deep voice, even before she saw the tall, broad figure and black hair. She looked up into Max Sarsby's glinting eyes and spoke coolly.

'I'm a rep, not a skier. My job's down here on the ground.'

He raised his dark brows. 'You mean you don't ski? Not at all? I'm amazed that you do the job, then. Surely you need to know what your guests are doing? Don't you ever feel you want to have a go?'

Kate hesitated. He had gained quite the wrong impression from what she'd said, but did it really matter?

Nobody here knew that she skied, or knew anything about what had happened to her. That was the way she wanted it. And anyway, it was true in a way—she *didn't* ski. Not any more.

'I'm quite happy doing my job,' she said briefly. 'And it keeps me quite busy enough—I wouldn't have much time for skiing, even if I wanted to.'

His look told her that he didn't believe her—anyone could make time for skiing if they really wanted to. And there was a touch of contempt in his eyes, too, as if he thought anyone not interested in skiing must be lacking in something vital. Kate felt an itch of resentment. Well, it just went with Julie's assessment of him—that he was arrogant. So arrogant that he couldn't envisage a life other than the one he'd chosen for himself; couldn't believe that other people might have different ideas.

'If you want the ski bus, it's just coming,' she observed, beginning to walk along the village street.

Max Sarsby hefted his skis on to his other shoulder. They were extremely long skis, Kate noticed, towering well above his head—the skis of an expert. He looked down at her unsmilingly, and she found herself wishing that he would relax, as he had done once or twice with the Brunners. Julie was right—he did have an attractive smile then; it gave his rather sombre face an entirely different look, hinting at a personality that was normally concealed. Perhaps underneath his ruthlessness there was something quite different.

Watch it! she told herself sternly. You already know he's dangerous. Keep away!

And, to her relief, Max hadn't sought her company, either. But this morning he didn't seem inclined to let her go so easily.

'There'll be another bus along soon,' he said. 'What about a coffee? You've got a few minutes, haven't you—and we don't seem to get much chance to talk at the Brunners'.'

'I have to go to the information office——' Kate began, but to her astonishment he took her elbow between his fingers and, even through the thickness of his gloves and her jacket, she could feel the uncompromising strength of his grip.

She felt something else, too—a flare of sensation that warned her again that this man was dangerous.

'You've plenty of time for that,' he said in a pleasant tone that brought a shiver to her spine. 'And I shan't keep you long. I do want to catch the next bus. Now—shall we go into the Heigenhäuser or the tavern?'

Helplessly, Kate shook her head. What did it matter where they went? She had the strange feeling that she was being kidnapped in broad daylight. But that was ridiculous. She only had to pull away, refuse to go with him. . . She moved her arm experimentally, and immediately felt his fingers tighten.

'Half an hour isn't a lot to ask,' his deep voice murmured in her ear.

Inside the restaurant, it was warm and bright. The cleaners had finished their work, and already tables were laid for lunch. The smell of coffee permeated the air, together with the delicious scent of fresh bread and pastries from the baker's shop next door.

'Anything to eat?' Max asked, and Kate shook her head. He ordered two coffees, and then sat back and surveyed her.

'Well, I suppose you've had time to find out all about me now.'

His tone was friendly enough, even amused, but Kate's uneasiness immediately sharpened into resentment.

She flushed. 'Find out about you? What do you mean? Are you implying that I've been gossiping about you?'

Max Sarsby's black brows rose. His face changed, the easy smile hardening. 'Call it gossip, if you like,' he said, an edge to his voice, and she knew that her reaction had angered him. 'You didn't really know much about me when I arrived at the Brunners', did you? Only what young Dieter told you. But I'm willing to bet you've found out more since—from the other reps, most likely. No doubt you've all had your heads together and had a good old session about me—am I right?'

Kate felt her flush deepen. She remembered her talk with Julie on the way to Salzburg, only yesterday. But it had hardly been gossip. Her resentment increased, and she said sharply, 'Yes, as a matter of fact one of the other girls did tell me a little about you. But no more than I already knew. And if you think we've been holding gossip sessions, and telling each other how lucky we are to have the wonderful Max Sarsby among us— well, you're completely wrong. We've all got far too much to do.'

'Too much to find time for a little gossip?' he said sceptically. 'I find that hard to believe.'

'Oh, for heaven's sake!' Kate snapped. 'Surely even you aren't so arrogant that you think there's nothing else for people to talk about than what you're doing? Look, you may have moved in that sort of world before your accident—a world where everyone was out to win, and therefore vitally interested in each other as rivals. I suppose you were even interesting to a certain section of the Press and the public who were into competitive skiing. But it's different here. This is just a small resort, where people come mostly to *learn* to ski. They'll have heard of you, I'm sure—but they won't be following you around with their autograph albums and queuing up to touch the hem of your ski-jacket. If it's that kind of adulation you want, you should go to one of the more fashionable resorts—Kitzbühel or Verbier. There are plenty of Hooray Henrys there to hang on to your every word!'

Max stared at her for a few moments. His brows were drawn together in a heavy bar over his brilliant eyes. His jaw was tight, his mouth compressed. Kate took a sip of her coffee and met his look, determined not to be intimidated.

'And there speaks one who knows all about skiing,' he drawled at last, but she could hear the anger that was tamped down in his voice. 'Being an expert yourself, of course, you——'

'We're not talking about skiing,' Kate said tersely. 'We're talking about gossiping. About you.'

'And you don't deny that you *have* been talking about me. You and the other reps.' He moved impatiently. 'Good lord! I came here because it was the quietest place I knew with access to a good advanced skiing circuit. And what do I find? The place is seething with skiers— beginners, most of them, though I don't have any objection to that, at least it keeps them off the black runs—and twittering tour company reps with nothing better to do than sit around drinking coffee and dishing the dirt about any poor mutt who happens to come within their orbit! Look,' he went on forcibly, ignoring Kate's gasp of indignation, 'all I want is for you to make

sure the gossip stays within bounds. I don't want the
Press getting hold of the fact that I'm here, right? And I
don't want anyone following me around to see just what
I'm doing. If I find there is—I'll know who to blame.'
His eyes burned into Kate's as if he were trying to brand
her mind. 'Understand?'

Kate took a moment or two to swallow her fury
sufficiently to be able to speak. 'Do I understand?' she
said at last, fighting to keep her voice steady. 'Oh, yes,
Mr Sarsby, I understand all right. You think that
nobody's interested in anyone but you—you think we're
all watching with bated breath to see what wonderful
thing you'll do next. All right, I admit you've shown
enormous determination—enormous courage—to fight
your way back after the accident you had,' her voice
shook a little despite all her efforts, 'but it doesn't mean
you can expect admiration for the rest of your life. You
have to earn that, too, Mr Sarsby. And you won't earn
it by being insufferably arrogant. The world doesn't
revolve around you, any more than it does around me or
anyone else, and the sooner you learn that the better.
And it might just surprise you to know,' she went on,
picking up her jacket and searching blindly for the
sleeve, 'that I do have other things to do than talk to
you, and I haven't the slightest intention—and nor has
anyone else, as far as I know—of alerting the world
Press to the fact that you're here. Not that I imagine the
village would be invaded by foreign correspondents if I
did!' she finished bitingly, and thrust her hand into the
wrong arm-hole.

Max sat back, looking a little stunned. Then he
grinned at Kate's efforts to get her jacket on. Casually,
he reached across and pulled it off, holding it so that she

could not begin again. Angrily, she jerked at the material, but his hand covered hers, large and warm. Kate stopped at once; there was a moment of electric silence as she slowly raised her eyes and met the smouldering blue gaze opposite.

She swallowed a little.

'Let's start again, shall we?' Max said softly, and there was an odd note in his voice, an intentness that matched the sudden fleeting darkness of his gaze. 'Let's go right back to the beginning and start again.'

Kate struggled with herself. She wanted to refuse—wasn't there something she had to do? But the world had narrowed down to this tiny spot—she and Max Sarsby at a corner table in an otherwise empty restaurant—and she had a dreadful feeling that it was all inevitable, and that there was nothing she could do to prevent an inexorable chain of events. And she knew too that she had over-reacted. Her outburst had been quite unwarranted. But she could not—dared not—bring herself to apologise.

But. . .start again? Let this man pierce her defences, knowing just how dangerous he could be to her? She looked at him, at the navy-turquoise eyes, the black brows, the strength of the determined face with lips that could soften to a heart-melting smile. She looked down at his hand, still caressing hers, and felt the warm strength of it.

And suddenly another man's face swam before her eyes. A face that was quite different from Max Sarsby's—fair, almost boyish, yet still charged with that same ruthless strength, the implacable determination, the ambition that could destroy. . .

'Beginning?' she said, and her voice shook in spite of

her efforts to maintain it. 'I'm sorry, Mr Sarsby. What kind of a beginning could there ever be for us? And now, if you don't mind——' she tugged again at her jacket. '—I really do have to go. I have work to do.'

This time, Max Sarsby released her. His eyes were on her face, dark now, and veiled, his thoughts hidden. But his mouth was hard, and she knew that his anger had begun again.

She turned and hurried from the restaurant, knowing that she had not come out of the encounter well. Yet how else could she have dealt with it? Max Sarsby was danger, there was no doubt about that. A danger she wasn't prepared to face.

CHAPTER THREE

IF SHE had not been so busy herself, Kate might almost have suspected Max Sarsby of avoiding her.

But her own job took up almost all her time—there was always some little problem to be sorted out, some difficulty with accommodation or travel. Most of the guests were only too willing to enjoy themselves, making Kate's job relatively easy—but there was always the occasional one who seemed to take a delight in needling her, in presenting her with small, irritating problems that could, if not treated carefully, soon begin to loom large. One week, she had a group who seemed unusually fussy about their food, starting with two small boys who refused anything but chips, and including a vegetarian and a woman on a special diet. The special diet, which had been arranged beforehand, was easy enough, but the vegetarian had not specified any particular needs beforehand and his discontent, added to that of the two boys, spread through the whole group so that, by the end of the week, hardly a meal appeared to be acceptable and the hotel staff were becoming increasingly sullen.

Kate's other problems included injuries—fortunately there were few of these, but there was one week in which two guests wrenched their knees and one woman, who had come skiing with a friend who had to return home at the end of the week, had to be taken to hospital in Salzburg and kept in for several days until her husband could be flown out from England. This meant several

trips backwards and forwards for Kate, who found
herself creeping into her bed regularly in the small hours,
and sleeping until after the skiers had all left the village
for the main skiing area, which was a twenty-minute
bus-ride away. She then had all her normal hotel rounds
and paperwork to do, and by the end of the week felt
that she could do with a spell in a hospital bed herself—
if only for the peace and quiet.

It was not surprising that she saw little of Max during
this period, nor that when they did meet they should
pass with little more than a nod of acknowledgement.
Occasionally, in the night, she thought with a pang of
the touch of his long, tapering fingers and the intent look
in his dark, brilliant eyes. But then she would remind
herself of his terrifying ambition—ambition of the kind
that could wreck lives. No, she thought, quelling the
sensations that rose within her. No. Leave it alone. Once
was enough. And she would turn over and, exhausted,
fall blessedly asleep.

All the same, she did think quite a lot about the story
Julie had told her. He had said very little about his
injuries, or about his sufferings in hospital, but she knew
that they must have been considerable. And the cour-
ageous determination needed to fight back to health
from such a horrific situation made her feel ashamed.
All right, so she'd come to Austria, to the situation she
had herself feared—but was that enough? Oughtn't she
to try, at least, to overcome the last and greatest of her
own fears—to ski again? Wasn't that what, deep down,
she'd wanted to do all along, although she'd been afraid
to take that final step?

For a long time, Kate fought against the growing
knowledge that, if she were ever to find peace with

herself, she had at least to try. And it was the example
of Max Sarsby, who had battled against his own injuries
and won, that finally spurred her into action. How could
she be so cowardly? she scolded herself. She hadn't even
been injured herself. What right had she to cower safely
in the village streets when Max was going up there day
after day, forcing his body to forget, to do his will, to
bend to his own overwhelming, driving need?

Not that he would know, or even care, what she did.
He seemed to have forgotten their brief moment of
intimacy when his fingers had touched hers so lightly in
the restaurant.

Meanwhile, it seemed she was doomed to endure this
powerful physical awareness of him—an awareness that
refused to disappear. It was something she was quite
determined not to give way to—but how, in the mean-
time, could she lessen the discomfort it caused?

It was difficult to avoid a man forever, when you were
living in the same house with him.

On one day of each week, Kate arranged an excursion
to Salzburg. As usual, although most of the guests
wanted to do nothing else but ski, there were still a few
who took the opportunity of visiting the beautiful little
city. The halt and the lame, she described them to
herself, watching as the minibus was boarded by an
assortment of people: one or two cross-country skiers,
exhausted by the rigours of *langlauf*, a couple of non-
skiing wives, who were patently glad to be returning to
'civilisation' for a few hours, two beginners, who were
ruefully hobbling on wrenched knees, and an intermediate who had sprained a wrist falling on the icy pavement.
There were also a few who were having a fortnight's

skiing and taking a day off, but as the weather seemed determined to remain bright and sunny, with snow falling mostly at night, most people had opted to go out on the slopes again. And Kate had finally made up her mind to join them.

It was a pity she hadn't brought her own skis. Buying new ones, together with boots and goggles and a proper ski-suit, was an expense she could have done without. But she had made up her mind to follow Max's example and fight back against tragedy. And she didn't want to draw attention to herself by doing her shopping in St Joachim, where by now everyone knew her. Better to do it anonymously, in Salzburg. She still felt diffident about revealing that she was, after all, a skier, and a good one, too. After all, she'd probably spent more of her childhood on skis than Max himself had. But knowing that was a different matter from demonstrating just how much she had—or had not—retained.

The minibus pulled up in the car park, and the passengers dispersed. Now she had only to call in at her travel company's office, and the rest of the day was her own.

It was when she had chosen her skis and was waiting to have her bindings adjusted that she saw Max.

He was passing by, strolling slowly along the pavement outside the ski shop. Kate felt her heart leap, and drew back quickly into the shadows. Any skier would be bound to pause and look into the windows, and that was just what he did. And—worse still—he was accompanied by a woman.

Kate recognised her at once. It was Helga, the most beautiful and statuesque of the village ski instructors. Not a local girl, she came from Munich, and knew the ski area well. She had joined the ski-school only this year, and already most of the men instructors were half in love with her—together, Kate imagined, with most of the men in her classes. She combined a firm teaching attitude with a dazzling charm that would have almost any man at her feet.

Including Max Sarsby? Kate watched with mixed feelings. The German girl looked more stunning than ever today. She had exchanged her scarlet ski-suit for a short jacket in thick grey fur that came high around her chin. Her chestnut hair lay like a flame across the sumptuous fabric, and her dark eyes gleamed like those of a small, alert animal. Below the jacket she wore tight-fitting black leggings, which outlined the shapeliness of her long legs, partly encased in brilliantly polished black high-heeled boots.

The athletic ski instructor transformed into model-girl glamour, Kate thought wryly, never realising that her own height and figure more than matched that of Helga's, while her blonde hair shimmered in the winter sunshine like palest honey. For a few moments she watched as the couple paused outside the shop, considering the equipment displayed in the window. They looked so right together, she thought wistfully, his black head against her tawny one, his massive strength making her height look almost frail. And when she noticed Helga's hand curl into his, she felt a pang of loneliness that was almost too much to bear. Had he forgotten those moments when his fingers had caressed hers, so lightly yet so burningly? Or had it meant nothing at all to him?

A cough from behind her drew her back to the present, and she turned to find the ski mechanic holding out her

skis, neatly fitted now with bindings, her new boots
already slotted into place to demonstrate their correct
fit. She smiled and thanked him, taking out her purse to
pay and waiting while the skis were put into a long bag.
The minibus could call round this way to collect them
on the way back that afternoon, the assistant agreed,
and, while he busied himself making out the slip for
Kate's credit card, she glanced back at the window.

Max and Helga had gone. Whether or not they had
seen her, she had no idea. And she had more than a
suspicion that they were in no state to notice anyone
else, anyway.

It was probably just as well, she thought. She already
knew that Max was bad news for her. And he'd never
given any indication that he saw her as anything more
than a holiday rep, and a gossipy one at that! It should
have been a relief to see him with Helga.

So why did her heart ache so strangely?

By January the season was in full swing. The snow on
the ski-slopes was several feet deep; after a week of
blizzards immediately after Christmas, the weather had
cleared and the sun shone down from a blue sky on to
the glittering mountains. From nine in the morning,
when the lifts opened, until after they closed at five, the
pistes were a kaleidoscope of colour as skiers zigzagged
down the runs, and the air was filled with laughter.

Kate looked at her skis, still packed away in their long
yellow bag. She had still not gathered together enough
courage to use them, promising herself each day that she
would take the next opportunity and then postponing
the challenge yet again. But this morning she was
determined to overcome her fears, once and for all. It

was ridiculous to go on in this way, she scolded herself. She knew she could ski, didn't she? She'd been able to ski for as long as she'd been able to walk, hadn't she? So why was she dithering? Her parents certainly wouldn't have wanted her to stop. In fact, they'd have been downright furious with her for the way she was behaving.

As for Max Sarsby—well, look what *he'd* overcome. And although Kate didn't have an overwhelming ambition to spur her on, she was more and more aware that, for her, her own self-respect was very much involved—and that was more important than winning any glamorous trophy.

Her face set, Kate pulled on her new ski-boots. At least she'd had the sense to wear them in her room during the evenings, to get her feet accustomed to them, but even so they felt stiff and unwieldy as she stumped across the floor. She dragged the skis from their bag and stretched experimentally, holding them over her shoulder. They felt fine; so did her new jade-green one-piece suit. She checked the pockets quickly: goggles, sun-cream, money, lift-pass—yes, everything was there. She hesitated for one more moment, then took herself firmly in hand and steered the skis through the door.

And as she stepped out of the house, walked straight into Max.

Kate stopped, stifling a groan. She'd taken special care to make sure he was out of the house before she'd left. The one thing she didn't want was his eyes on her— why, she didn't really know, except that she still felt awkward about allowing him to think she couldn't ski, and because since that day in Salzburg, seeing him with Helga, she had been more confused than ever about her own feelings. She had known all too clearly just what kind of danger he represented to her; she ought to have been relieved that he found another woman attractive. Yet she couldn't prevent his face from coming into her mind when she least wanted it. She couldn't prevent that little leap of the heart whenever she knew he was in the Brunners' house, and that they might meet at any moment. She couldn't keep the thoughts of him from her mind as she lay in bed at night, longing for sleep and yet reluctant to let those thoughts go.

He was too damned attractive, she thought bitterly, and too easy to fall for. His sort of man—powerfully capable, strong and full of easy determination—seemed to be just the sort who attracted her, and she knew from experience what was the other side of that particular coin—blinkered and total self-centredness.

It wouldn't be quite so bad if such men seemed at all vulnerable. But they never did. That moment in the restaurant had been an illusion, nothing more. And as she looked up into Max's steel-blue eyes, and noted the grim set of his mouth, the thought of any kind of vulnerability seemed ludicrous.

'And just where are you off to?' he demanded.

Kate faced him.

'Well, I was thinking of trying a little windsurfing, but the tide's out, so I——'

'Cut the jokes,' he broke in. 'I thought you didn't ski? That's what you told me, right?'

'Yes, but——'

'So you've decided to give it a go? Well, that's all right—but why aren't you joining the beginners' class? You don't, I hope, imagine that it's possible to just clip on a pair of skis and go?'

'I'd be rather stupid to imagine that,' Kate rejoined

coolly, 'since I spend most of my working hours listening to people who are finding it quite different.'

'So what are you planning to do? Take the bus and the chair-lift to the top of the mountain and just slide down, to see how it feels?' His eyes raked her with scorn, and then travelled up to the tips of her skis. 'Good lord! Where on earth did you get those?'

'In Salzburg. If you'd just let me——'

'You mean you just went into a shop in Salzburg and bought a pair of skis? Without ever having tried before?' He reached up and touched the curved tips. 'These must be all of two hundred centimetres! And they're far too stiff for a beginner. Didn't you take any advice? With all these ski instructors around, didn't you think to ask anyone what you ought to have? Even if you refused to ask me, you should have asked *someone*.'

'I do know about ski lengths,' Kate said coldly. 'I spend a good deal of time in the ski shop every week, helping people to choose the right skis and boots. I know about weight and experience, too. You don't have to be an expert skier to understand straightforward things like that.'

'But you do have to be an expert skier—or a pretty good one, at least—to use skis like the ones you're carrying,' he pointed out. 'Look, just take it from me—you'd be crazy to go out on a pair of skis like that if you've never even tried it before. I'm not trying to interfere or bully you, Kate—I just don't want to see you getting yourself injured, that's all.'

Kate sighed. She knew that he was right—if she had been a beginner, it would have been foolhardy in the extreme to go out alone on the mountain on any skis, let alone the ones she had bought. And it wasn't his fault he thought she was a beginner—she'd given him that impression from the start, and allowed him to go on thinking it.

'Look, I'm sorry,' she said. 'I've let you think I've never skied before—but I have. Not lately, but I did ski when I was younger and——'

Before she could finish, he interrupted again, no less impatiently than before.

'You mean you came on a school skiing holiday, I suppose! Well, that hardly makes you an expert. All right, so you may have passed beginners' stage about eight or nine years ago—but you'll find it's very different when you get up on the high slopes, and as for going alone, you're crazy even to think of it. Look——' he pulled back the wrist of his jacket and glanced at his watch '—I just came back to make a phone call. Hang on for me, will you? I'll take you up on one of the easier runs. If you're determined to be foolhardy, there's not much anyone can do about it, but at least I can see that you don't get killed!'

He marched into the house, leaving Kate staring after him and seething with indignation. So he still thought she was a beginner! He hadn't even bothered to listen to her when she'd begun to explain. All right, so he *wanted* to have the wrong idea. And what's more, he thought he could order her around, did he? Sit her here like an obedient dog, tell her to 'stay' and then, with all the patronising condescension that was the most maddening thing about him, take her up on one of the 'easy' runs? How very, very kind of him! And how very, very surprised he was going to be when he found that she'd dared to go off without him.

Kate shouldered her skis and marched off along the

pavement, her boots crunching on the previous night's new fall of snow. Her breath misted and froze on the icy air, but inside her thick, downy ski-suit and gloves she was cosily warm. Her head was protected by a cap which matched her suit; she had wound her hair up on top of her head, and round her neck was a soft white scarf.

The ski bus was trundling along the street towards her. Kate waved, and it stopped. The driver leaned down and grinned cheerily.

'A nice day for skiing, *Fräulein*. Just stack your skis at the back.'

Kate smiled at him and did as she was told, then scrambled aboard. The bus was half-empty—most of the skiers had already gone up the steep, winding road to the mountain. The early buses were always crammed with intermediate and advanced ski-school pupils, eager to try their skills on the red and black runs that criss-crossed the steep slopes, and many of the skiers who came solo had their own cars which they parked by the first chair-lift.

As the bus pulled away again, Kate saw Max come out of the Brunners' house and glance up and down the road. He stared after the bus and she ducked quickly out of sight. Not that there was a thing he could do about it, even if he did see her!

She settled back into her seat, feeling comfortably anonymous. None of the other passengers knew her— they were either the guests of another company, or day visitors from another town. She listened vaguely to the conversations around her, and thought about Max.

Now that she had escaped him, she felt slightly uneasy about her flight. After all, brusque and patronising though he'd been, he had meant well. He thought she was a beginner, and had been genuinely concerned under his irritation. And he'd been prepared to take her up on the mountain himself and look after her.

Maybe she oughtn't to have run off like that. He might be really worried now—thinking of her alone up there, not knowing which runs to use, slithering into danger, helpless without him.

But I'm not helpless without him, Kate reminded herself sternly. I'm an experienced skier—I've skied all my life, just as he has. And if he doesn't know that—so what? I'm not answerable to him. If he wants to worry about me, that's his problem, not mine.

She gazed out of the window. The bus was winding slowly up a series of hairpin turns. Deep in the valley below, she could see fir trees, frozen cascades, even a few deer. Above, the sky was a strong, dense blue, and the whiteness of the snow had everyone putting on sunglasses and goggles.

As she slipped her own over her face, Kate saw a car overtaking the bus on one of the straighter stretches. Two pairs of skis were strapped to the roof. And as it passed she saw a face turned up towards her, scanning the rows of faces at the window.

Max. Somehow he'd managed to get a lift. And she knew, without any shadow of a doubt, that when she got off the bus he would be waiting for her.

The brilliant light seemed to dim. And the trepidation that settled over Kate's heart amounted almost to a premonition of doom.

CHAPTER FOUR

MAX was, indeed, waiting for Kate as she descended from the bus. His face was grimmer than she had ever seen it, his jaw tight, and his eyes flint-hard. She took one look at him and knew that he was very angry indeed.

And justifiably so, she acknowledged as she met his look. But then she reminded herself again that she hadn't *asked* him to worry about her. She lifted her chin and challenged him with her own green eyes.

'Taken to hitch-hiking in your old age?' she asked cheekily. 'I thought that was just for the kids.'

'You know very well why I'm here,' he growled. 'And if anyone's acting childishly around here, it isn't me. Now—for the last time, will you think again about using those skis?' He watched as she removed them from the rack at the back of the bus. 'I've told you, they're far too long for a beginner—even for an intermediate. You'd need to have quite a lot of skiing experience under your belt before you graduated to skis that length, and——'

'And *I've* told *you*,' Kate rejoined calmly, 'that I *have* skied before. Not that I have to tell you anything. You're not my keeper. I'm a grown woman, and I make my own decisions as to what I do. And I've decided to go skiing. This morning. With these particular skis. So, if you'll please move out of my——'

'Kate!' There was a new note in his voice, a note of real concern, and Kate could not decry it. She hesitated, turning back to him, and found him staring at her with

47

an expression that turned her heart over. It was gone at once, so quickly that she thought she'd imagined it—but it had had its effect on her, and when he spoke again she could not find it in her heart to rebuff him.

'Then let me come with you, Kate. Let's ski together. Just for a while. Just to set my mind at rest.' His eyes were on her, sending her messages she dared not interpret. 'Please.'

That last little word was her undoing. Silently, she handed him her sticks to hold while she fastened her skis. Then she waited while he clipped his own bindings tight. They slid towards the chair-lift side by side.

As soon as they were settled in the two-man seat, soaring towards the white peaks, Max said, 'I'm beginning to think you've been holding out on me, Kate. You got on this lift as if you'd been doing it all your life. Most holiday skiers are still a bit nervous of them after several years, first time out.'

'And how would you know?' Kate asked tartly. 'I doubt if you've been within spitting distance of a holiday skier for years.'

Max laughed. 'Oh, come on—I have to queue for lifts like everyone else when I'm not racing. I've rubbed shoulders with them all—from the little tots who seem to have been born on skis, to the absolute dunce who'll never learn even to stand up. I'm not quite such an élitist as you seem to think.'

Kate said nothing. She was all too conscious of the fact that he was rubbing shoulders with her now. Rubbing more than that, too—she could feel the length of him, from shoulder to ankle, burning against her, even through the thickness of their ski-suits. She gazed fixedly at the view, wondering how she had come to be in this position.

The chair-lift rose steadily up the mountain. All around them, the view was extending with every yard they ascended; a view of white peaks, stretching away on every side. Peaks that were clothed on their lower slopes with dark pine trees, the gleaming snow emerging from their depths in a sweep of brilliant light. In the distance she could see the runs, with a pattern of skiers flowing down like a bright cascade. Below, sometimes almost close enough to touch, were the lowest *pistes* leading back to the car park. One of the big 'rat-track' machines was making its way up, flattening down the soft, powdery snow, and there were ski-tracks over the roof of a half-buried hut to show that someone had daringly skied right over it to jump to the powder snow on its far side. Kate remembered having done just such a thing herself, when skiing with her parents and her friends.

'Look. There's one of the black runs.' Max moved closer to her and slipped an arm round her shoulders to direct her gaze over to the left. 'That bumpy area is caused by people turning—we call them moguls. They're quite a challenge to ski. Mogul-bashing—you'll have heard people talking about it, I dare say.'

'Yes, I have, once or twice,' Kate agreed demurely. He *still* hadn't taken in that she was an experienced skier! Seething, she made up her mind to surprise him.

Meanwhile, she was forced to sit in this chair-lift, her body held closely and firmly against his. The ascent took a quarter of an hour—fifteen minutes during which Kate was aware of very little more than his body against hers, his warmth, vitality and sheer masculinity throbbing beside her, so that her own muscles felt weak and trembling under his spell. And when they finally reached the station and glided off to the top of the runs, she did not know whether to be glad or sorry that it was over.

She skied easily over to the slope which led down the first run, and looked down.

This was the moment that had haunted her dreams and all too often turned them into nightmares. It was this moment she had imagined: the moment when she stood at the top of a run and let herself go. The exhilaration of it. . .and then the horror. Both had been only too real.

For a few seconds, panic overwhelmed her. She struggled with her desire to turn back, abandon her skis and go back down in the chair-lift. If she had been alone, she might have done it. But Max Sarsby was there, his eyes sardonically fixed on her, and she knew he sensed her indecision. And although she also knew that he misunderstood its reasons, she refused to give him the satisfaction of thinking himself proved right.

'Look a bit frightening, does it?' he drawled, and the anger that Kate felt was all the spur she needed.

'Frightening?' she said coolly. 'Not in the least. Let's go, shall we?'

She gave herself a small push with her sticks and felt the skis bite into the snow as she began a gentle traverse. Max was following her—somewhat taken aback, she guessed, since he'd clearly expected to lead. No doubt he would try to overtake her as they progressed down the slope, and with a wicked impishness she determined not to let him.

She came to the end of her traverse and transferred her weight to her left ski. Automatically, the ski turned;

she planted her pole in just the right spot, lifted her right ski briefly to complete the turn, and began to traverse again. A feeling of pleasure began slowly to warm her body, and she glanced down the slope, judging its shape and its steepness. The easy movement seemed to flow through every muscle, so that she began to feel a part of the long, slender skis with their gently curved tips. She turned again, delighting in the smoothness, and suddenly all her fear and panic disappeared. She was skiing again, as if nothing had ever happened to make her vow that she never would. All the irresolution and worry of the past months had disappeared, and there was nothing but the enchantment and exhilaration of being on the snow again. It was as easy as that.

Now Kate began to concentrate entirely on her skiing, challenging herself to make the best of every swooping turn, to perfect each long traverse. She leaned forwards, aware of nothing but the snow and the slope in relation to her own progress. Weight, pole, turn, weight, pole turn. The words echoed through her brain, as they had done when she was a child, remembering her father's voice as he encouraged her down a new run. And then even they faded and disappeared, and she was skiing as naturally as if she had been born doing it, as if the snow were her natural element and her feet made to be two hundred centimetres long.

At the bottom of the run, she turned into an uphill christie to execute a neat stop, and looked back.

Max was close behind her. He came in beside her and halted. He turned towards her.

'All right, Kate. You're no beginner, I can see that. So why did you pretend you were? And just how advanced are you?'

Kate looked back at him. The deep blue of the sky was reflected in his dark glasses. She could see tiny views of the mountains all around, and she could see her own face. She knew that she would have to answer his questions, but she didn't want to yet. Not when she had only just rediscovered the joys of skiing.

'Let's do some more first,' she said, hearing the tremor of eagerness in her voice. 'I want to get right up on the top—do something really exciting. And I assure you, I can do it—you don't have to worry any more! And then we'll have some lunch somewhere, and I'll tell you anything you want to know.'

Max looked searchingly into her face, and she knew that he still doubted her. And why shouldn't he? she thought with sudden compunction. She had given him little reason to suppose she would ever confide in him, even when he had revealed himself to her. She hadn't ever intended to, after all. She had never meant to let him get that close to her.

But now, after just a few minutes on the slopes, everything was different. It was as if the slate had been wiped clean—as clean as the pure white mountains which surrounded them. Her mind had been cleared and she could talk freely about what had happened. And she wanted to. She wanted to talk, and she wanted to talk to Max.

Just what this meant, she did not analyse. Her exhilaration was too great to allow her to consider the more disturbing implications.

She gave Max a flashing smile. 'Let's go down to the next lift and then take the big chair up to the top. There's a wonderful mogul-field there, I've heard—no doubt you've been down it—and I'm dying to try it out for myself. Mogul-bashing, I believe they call it—isn't that what you told me?'

Max stared at her and then his tanned face split into a broad grin.

'You little minx!' he said, and for the first time since Kate had known him there was a laugh in his voice. It made him unbearably attractive, and she wanted suddenly to fling herself into his arms and be hugged, to hug him back in an effort to express all that she was feeling on this sparkling and joyous morning. But even as she moved he was turning away, and she gave the little push that was all that was necessary to set herself in motion again.

'You go first,' he said as she came level with him. 'I want to watch your style—it's quite a revelation. We'll *wedeln* down this next section, and then there's a good long *schuss* to the lift. And then I'll see just how good you are at mogul-bashing!' Kate gathered speed and flew ahead of him. The wind raced past her ears, freezing her cheeks as she went into the swaying rhythm of the *wedeln*. There was nobody else on the slope; with Max behind her, she could have been alone at the top of the world.

But, wherever she was, she knew he was very close. And she could hear his amused chuckles as he muttered, over and over again, in time with the rhythm of their skiing, 'Beginner, indeed! Just you wait until I get you off those skis, Kate Markham. Beginner, indeed. . .just you wait. . .'

Kate felt a thrill that had nothing at all to do with skiing. And everything to do with another kind of danger.

* * *

'You mean,' Max said slowly, staring at her, 'that they were both killed?'

Kate nodded. She stared down at her mug of *glühwein*, fighting back the tears that still came to her eyes every time she thought of that terrible day. It had been a mistake to think she could talk to Max about it, she thought. The memory was still too sharp. And alongside it now was a miserable guilt that she had just spent an enjoyable morning skiing again.

Max's hand covered her own. It was large and warm and gentle, but she could feel the strength that lay dormant in it. She wanted badly to turn her own hand over under his, to let her fingers curl into his palm as they ached to do. But another memory intruded—the memory of Helga, outside the ski shop in Salzburg, standing close to Max with her hand curled into his. And she reminded herself, too, of his ruthless ambition, and what it could mean to any woman unfortunate enough to love him. She didn't need that—not on top of everything else that had happened to her.

She swallowed and looked up at him, flicking back her blonde hair and pinning a smile to her face. 'It's all right. I'm over it now—most of the time. But, as you can guess, that's why I wasn't too keen on skiing again. Apart from anything else—well, it is a reminder.'

'I should think it is! I'm amazed you ever plucked up the courage.' There was a warm admiration in his eyes, and Kate looked down again quickly. Max hesitated and then added quietly, 'Do you feel you can talk about it? Tell me exactly what happened?'

And suddenly, with his warm hand covering hers in the corner of the mountain restaurant, with the wide windows looking out at the shining peaks, and the other skiers chattering cheerfully around them, Kate felt that she could.

After all, Max and she would be together for only a very short time. The season would last for only a few weeks now; he would be leaving the mountains when the snow began to melt, and she would be going to another resort—one that was busy in the summer and attracted a different kind of holiday-maker. They would never see each other again after these few brief weeks.

Why not tell him? Why not let it all pour out?

'We were glacier-skiing,' she said, speaking in a low voice, almost as if to herself. 'My two cousins, Jane and Peter, and I. We'd done it before, often—I lived most of my childhood in Switzerland, you see, and they spent their holidays with us. My father taught us all to ski as soon as we could walk. He loved to go off-*piste* and ski the wild places, and my mother was as good a skier as he was. There was nothing they couldn't tackle. And although he's not strong enough to ski now, he liked us to tell him about the runs we made.'

'So you went glacier-skiing,' he prompted her as she fell silent, remembering those long days on the mountains with the cousins who were more like brother and sister to her: laughing, dark-haired Peter, so tall and broad, and tiny, blonde Jane. Together, they had shared so much laughter and excitement, infected with each other's high spirits. But the optimism and zest had left her for a long time after the accident, and only lately she had begun to feel it creeping back, tingling like the blood flowing back into frozen limbs, and equally painful.

She drew her hand away from Max's.

'Yes. Peter wanted to try a new route. It should have been safe enough. He'd flown over it before—a glacier,

not too high, and sweeping right down into the village.
The local guides had tried it, and thought it should
become a popular route for advanced skiers.' She closed
her eyes, remembering the helicopter flight they had
taken on that blue, sunny morning, the three of them
laughing and excited at the prospect of the adventure
ahead. The noise of the engine and the whirr of the
rotor-blades overhead sounded again in her mind, and
once more she could see the village dropping away
beneath them, the steep sides of the mountain rising all
around them and, finally, the broad, blue-white sweep
of the glacier below, a smooth white surface of unmarked
snow.

'The helicopter dropped us on the ridge,' she said,
looking at Max. 'I can't tell you how wonderful it
looked—that great white expanse of powder snow
stretching away below us. It wasn't straight all the way,
of course—it curved and twisted out of sight down the
mountain, behind huge boulders and under crags.'

And that was where the danger had been, unnoticed
by any of them as the helicopter flew its steady path up
the mountain. A vast accumulation of snow, poised over
a great crag—sliding gently, perhaps, even at that
moment, waiting until the three skiers should pass
directly in its path. . .

'I've never known such an exhilarating morning,' she
said quietly. 'I didn't want it to end—ever. I just wanted
it to go on and on.'

She was silent again, reliving those moments when
she had seemed to be above the world, lifted into some
magical realm where the air was rare and light, and her
body could achieve an almost flying skill, swooping

down the endless slope, aware of nothing but the movement, the grace, and the cold wind of speed against her cheeks. The figures of Jane and Peter just ahead, brilliant in their sun-gold ski-suits, had had an almost ethereal look about them, that same other-worldliness that she'd sensed in herself, and she had known then that this was a moment she would remember all her life.

And then, cruelly, the moment had been struck away and shattered, as icicles were shattered from the roofs when they grew too long.

Kate had been aware of the danger first as a faint, distant rumbling—a vibration more than a sound. In her delight, she had ignored the implication, and then, as the noise had grown and swelled around her, and become a relentless thundering that echoed among the peaks and valleys of the mountain, she had snapped back into consciousness and alarm had flooded through her body.

Avalanche.

Her cousins had heard it, too. She saw them hesitate in their smooth, flowing rhythm. Peter paused, glanced around, and then upwards. Jane, too, raised her head. And Kate followed their eyes and saw what they saw.

She never knew whether she screamed or not. The sound would have been lost in the roar of the snow that was hurtling down the steep slope towards them. She remembered only an image of the white, murderous mass, the evil black rocks that it was bringing with it. She remembered only that she was far enough behind to escape the worst of it, being merely knocked over and swept for what was even so a frightening distance before coming to a breathless, half-buried stop in a great pile of roughened snow. She only knew that her last sight of her cousins had been of two sun-gold figures struggling momentarily against the onslaught before being carried inexorably down the mountain, and disappearing in a powdery white-out that rose like a cloud of doom somewhere deep in the valley.

As she finished talking, her voice dried, and she took a painful sip of *glühwein*. Her throat ached with tears, and she knew that when she was back in her room she would cry. But not here—not with all these other skiers, so happily oblivious of her pain, not with Max Sarsby.

She had been keeping her hands under the table, clenched tightly together between her knees. Now, as she set down the pottery mug, Max leaned across and captured her hand in both of his. His eyes were on her face, dark and intent.

'Thank you for telling me, Kate,' he said, his voice low and vibrant. 'I appreciate what it must have cost you. It's never easy to talk of these things, but I'm glad you did. . .I imagine the helicopter found you?'

She nodded, glad to speak of practicalities. 'The pilot was back at base by then, but he heard the roar and came straight up. He knew we must have been in its path. He picked me up and took me back, but we couldn't see any sign of my cousins. And it was much, much later when they finally found them.'

There was another silence, but this time Kate did not try to draw away from Max. She sat quite still, her hand under his, conscious of the warmth and strength that flowed from him. After a moment, she turned her hand over and their palms met.

'Your father,' Max said at last. 'I never connected it before—but he is John Markham, isn't he? The conductor?'

'Yes,' Kate said on a sigh. 'Yes, he is.'

'I remember hearing about his illness,' Max said soberly. 'He's a great loss to millions who love music.'

'Yes,' she said.

'And your cousins?' he asked. 'Were they your only family? No brothers or sisters?'

'No. And Peter and Jane's parents died years ago— that's why they spent so much time with us. We lived a strange life. My father was in demand for conducting all over the world, and he always took my mother and me with him. Until I went to school, that is. He was based in Geneva, of course—that was the easiest place for him to live, within reach of the orchestra he was resident with, and of the airport for the travelling he did. When I was old enough I went to boarding school in England with Jane, and then my mother went with him. But we always spent a lot of the winter together, skiing. He made sure of that. We went ski-touring a lot. I think there was hardly a mountain he didn't know.'

'And now it's all over for him—the skiing,' Max said quietly, and then, with force, 'Life is a harsh thing, Kate. Your father, who can give so much pleasure, too frail now to work, even to play. . .your cousins, killed.' He paused. 'It's different for me. Broken bones can be mended. When I had my accident, I was determined from the start that I was going to get better—ski again. I was determined that I *would* win that trophy. And I never gave up.'

Kate looked at him. His face was set in the hard, ruthless lines that had already touched her with fear, and now struck a new discord in her heart. How could a mere trophy matter so much? Particularly when you had already come close to death in its pursuit? Yet it was his

own example that had forced her back to the slopes
again. And having told her story, she found her mind
clearing once more, and knew that her cousins would
not have wished her to give up the sport that they had
all loved so much; they would have wanted her to go
ahead and enjoy it again.

Enjoy it, yes. But make it an end in itself? She looked
at Max's face and shook her head slightly. The grip of
his fingers felt suddenly cold and she took her hand
away quickly.

'What is it?' he asked. 'What's the matter, Kate?'

'Nothing,' she said, and smiled at him. 'I've just
noticed that my *glühwein* is finished. Can I get you some
more?'

He raised his eyebrows slightly and then grinned. 'A
liberated woman, I see! But no more *glühwein*—I'll have
coffee this time. And then we'll take another trip up to
the top of the mountain, shall we, and have an afternoon
on the moguls? Or do you think you've had enough for
one day?'

Kate felt that, in one way, she had indeed had more
than enough. But an afternoon's hard skiing, which
would take all her concentration, could be just what she
needed. And she heard again her father's laughter as he
encouraged her down the slopes.

'No, I'm fine,' she said. 'And maybe I'll even be able
to teach you a trick or two.'

It was unlikely, though, she thought as she made her
way through the throng of skiers to the counter. Max
Sarsby knew every trick in the book. He must be quite
well aware of the effect he had on her. And after today,
grateful though she might be for these few hours
together, she would keep well clear of him.

Not because she didn't like him. But because she knew now, with a clarity that was as cold as the snowy peaks surrounding them, that she could all too easily love him.

CHAPTER FIVE

'KATE. I want to talk to you.'

Kate started, and caught at the banister at the top of the stairs. It was dimly lit there, the soft light little more than a mellow glow on the wood-panelled walls. She had not realised, when she left her room, that there was anyone else in the house; it had been silent for a long time since Frau Brunner had called out a cheery goodbye and left to visit her sister in St Johann. She had had no idea that Max might be there, waiting to pounce on her.

'What on earth are you doing?' she demanded sharply. 'Lurking about in the shadows. . .I could have fallen from top to bottom.'

'I'm sorry, I didn't intend to frighten you.' He didn't sound in the least apologetic. He came forward, out of the dark corner in which he'd been standing, and his hand covered hers on the newel post. 'I've been waiting for you to come out. I've hardly seen you, these past two weeks.'

'You can hardly see me now,' Kate retorted, uncomfortably aware of his nearness, of the warmth of the hand that trapped her own. 'Why don't Austrians have brighter lights. . .? Look, I'm really in rather a hurry, Max, so if you don't mind. . .'

'But I do mind.' He was much too close now, his breath warm on her cheeks. 'And I don't really think you're in such a hurry as you like to pretend, sweet

Kate. After all, it's your day off, isn't it? Were you thinking of going skiing?'

'As a matter of fact, I am.' She paused. 'Alone.'

'Then you won't be keeping anyone waiting if we have a little talk first.' With a sudden movement, he swung open the door of his room and caught Kate around the shoulders, drawing her inside before she had time to protest. 'I should think we'd be private enough in here, wouldn't you?'

Kate's instinctive reaction was that it was a damned sight too private. But she bit back the words, determined to play this cool, not to give Max any inkling that the situation might be in any way beyond her control. Slowly, she lifted one hand to push back her shimmering hair and looked around the room.

'So this is Dieter's hideout,' she remarked. 'I must say, I think it's very generous of him to let you use it. The room he's got now is hardly more than a cupboard. But I suppose it's worth it to him, to have his idol living in the same house.'

'Hardly his idol. He'd rather an Austrian won the World Cup any day.'

'But you are one of the greats, aren't you?' Kate said coolly. 'And half Austrian, at that. I can understand a young boy like Dieter being impressed.'

'Meaning you're not?' Max took a step towards her. 'Kate, what's wrong? Since that day we skied together, you've done your level best to avoid me. Why?'

'I haven't at all,' she denied, too quickly. 'I've just been busy. You know what my job's like—there are all kinds of problems, and this past week or two——'

'You haven't even eaten here in that time,' he broke

in, ignoring her words. 'Frau Brunner's beginning to think you don't like her cooking, and——'

'I told her when I came that I'd eat most of my meals in the hotels. I like to keep in close contact with the guests, and I've got people in three different hotels, plus a few in snow homes, and some in apartments. It's a lot to look after. You don't understand——'

'No, I don't believe I do,' he said grimly. 'That day we were up on the mountain together, I thought I sensed something between us, Kate—something that could be good. I'd had an inkling of it before—when we talked in the Heigenhäuser that first morning. But skiing with you and talking to you—well, I imagined you felt it, too.' He reached out and gripped her hand. 'I still think I was right, Kate. There *is* something—something that only needs developing. But you don't want it to develop, do you? That's why you've been keeping out of my way. *Why?*'

Kate twisted her hand in his, but his grip only tightened on her fingers. Immediately, the guilt that she'd begun to feel at his words sharpened into anger. How dared he hold her like this—like a prisoner? She felt the angry flush brighten her cheeks as she shook back her hair and looked fearlessly up into his eyes.

'Let go of me, Max Sarsby! Who do you think you are? I don't have to justify my actions to you. So we had a good day together—and so I talked too much. Does that put me under some kind of obligation? Does it give you some kind of *right* over me? Don't you have any sense of delicacy?' Her voice broke a little. 'It wasn't easy, talking to you about that time, you know. And since then—well, I just haven't wanted to be reminded.'

Even as she spoke, she felt shame wash over her at the

way she was using her cousins' accident to cover up her real feelings. Her eyes fell under his stare and she felt her colour deepen.

But Max was clearly not deceived.

'Don't give me that!' he said harshly. 'Yes, I do have some delicacy—enough to be able to tell when you're not being sincere, and I might tell you I don't think much of the way you're trying to wriggle out of what is clearly your own problem. It's not worthy of you, Kate. What's wrong with plain honesty? Don't I warrant that?'

Kate lifted her head and looked up at him again. His eyes were smouldering, the flame-blue of a burning log that had been soaked in salt water. She looked into their depths and saw a message in them—a message only she could read. Her heart kicked against her ribs, then began a slow, heavy pounding. She opened her mouth to speak, but no words came. Instead, her lips formed no more than a tiny gasp and then stayed parted.

'Kate. . .' he muttered, deep in his throat, and bent his head to hers.

Kate struggled only briefly in the seconds before his lips touched her mouth. And then she was conscious of nothing but the feel of him: the softness of his kiss, deepening to warm passion as he drew her into his arms and tightened them around her; the hardness of his body as he pressed her close, so that her contours folded against him, fitting with the completeness of a distant horizon laid against curving hills. The room reeled around her as she closed her eyes and gave herself up to his velvety insistence, to the surging desire of her own body. A fiery heat spread itself from somewhere deep in her abdomen, up through her already swelling breasts and into her heart. She gasped again as the flames licked through her, tingling their way to her palms, her fingers, her toes, and she curled herself against him, clinging as if to a rock on some sheer and icy precipice, feeling the world falling away from beneath her feet.

With a desperation that came from many nights of longing, she took and returned his kisses, letting his mouth open hers, welcoming the intrusion of his tongue, the sharpness of his teeth as they nipped gently at her inner lips. With an urgency she'd been aware of only dimly, she let her hands move over his body as his were moving over her—seeking, exploring, drawing out a passion that she had never before suspected. It took control of her body, of her mind, of every deep emotion, sweeping her out of the world she had always believed she lived in, thrusting her into a realm she had barely even dreamed of. The roaring in her ears she translated as the roar of a thousand cascades, the thundering of her heart as the rejoicing of the mountains themselves. She felt his caresses as the sensuous warmth of a tropical breeze, and wanted only that they should be whispering over naked flesh, with nothing between the sensitive touch of his fingertips and the urgent response of her skin.

'Kate,' he muttered against her mouth. 'Kate, oh, Kate. . .' And she felt his lips move along the line of her jaw, down the length of her arched neck and into the hollow of her throat. As her hands moved to clasp his shoulders, she felt his fingers at the neck of her skiing sweater, unfastening the zip to release the polo collar, and then moving down to stroke the cleft between her breasts. She moaned a little and sought his lips again, and with a swift movement Max lifted her into his arms and laid her on his bed.

Kate lay quietly for a moment, looking up as he knelt beside the bed, his face level with hers. She turned her head slightly to meet his eyes, and felt something deep within her twist and flare as she caught the depth of passion in the dilated pupils, the ring of flaming blue. She could feel the rapid thunder of her heartbeat, the tremor of her limbs and, insistent through all her most sensitive and secret parts, the overpowering desire to be in his arms again, held hard against the lean maleness of him, giving herself with all the abandoned fire that she had kept hidden so deeply for so long.

'Kate. . .' he whispered again, and touched her cheek with his fingertips.

Kate turned her face into his palm. It was almost more than she could bear—this desperate need of him, the knowledge of what they could be together. But reason was beginning to seep back into her mind and she knew that she dared let this go no further—already it had gone much further than she had ever intended. If one kiss could do this. . . She turned back and met his eyes again, feeling the warm tears fill her own so that his face wavered and blurred before her, and she reached up with her own fingers to touch his cheek as he had touched hers.

'I'm sorry, Max,' she whispered. 'I shouldn't have let that happen. We've got to stop now, Max—we've got to forget we ever came together in that way. Let me go— please.'

He stared at her, his brows drawn together in a hard black line over his smouldering eyes. Disbelief brought new lines to his face as he slowly shook his head; and his hand, falling away from her cheek, found her shoulder and tightened on it almost cruelly.

'Stop?' he echoed harshly. 'Forget? Kate, what sort of a game is this to play? What in hell's name are you talking about? Don't tell me you're going to turn out to be a tease—because I simply won't believe it!'

'I'm not teasing you,' she said quietly, still fighting her own frantic instincts. 'I mean it, Max. Let me go now, and let's forget it ever happened. That's all I'm asking.'

'*All?*' The word burst from him with a violence that had her shaking and cowering on the bed. 'That's *all?* Kate, you don't know what you're saying. Look, I never meant it to happen—not like that, not so soon. I wasn't hanging about waiting to jump on you the moment we were alone in the house. I never intended to "take advantage" of you. But you know as well as I do, there's a chemistry between us that can't be denied. It hit you as hard as it did me, Kate. Don't try to say it didn't. Don't deny it. I'm not a complete fool.'

'I won't deny it.' Her green eyes were steady on his. 'Yes, Max, there was something. *Is* something, if you must have it. I don't behave like that with every man who makes a pass at me. As a matter of fact, I've never behaved like that with any man—and that doesn't mean I'm totally without experience, either. But—I daren't let it go any further, Max. It's as simple as that. It—it scares me. It's too much—too powerful. And besides that—it wouldn't work.'

'Wouldn't work? What wouldn't work, for heaven's sake? It seemed to me to be working very well indeed.'

Kate bit her lip and turned her face away. What was she to say to this man? He had offered her nothing— only a kiss. What did *he* want? An afternoon's dalliance? An affair to add spice to the rest of the skiing season?

Nothing he had said had indicated that he wanted any more than that. Perhaps, she thought bitterly, she ought to be liberated enough to accept that as an end in itself. But she knew that, having once given herself to this man, she would want more. And any deeper commitment was impossible.

'I'm not into casual affairs,' she said at last.

'And you think that's all this would be?'

'Well, it has to be, doesn't it? Look at the difference between us—you're a ski champion, or very nearly, and that's what you mean to be as soon as you possibly can. You're out there every day, training, doing exercises, skiing the hardest runs you can find, getting yourself fit for next year's competitions. You don't want a permanent relationship. And if you did, it would hardly be with a mere holiday rep—not when you've got all the most glamorous women on the slopes at your feet. Women who'd gladly give up everything to follow you around the world to all the best skiing areas. No, Max, you can't pretend you want me for anything more than an affair—I just won't believe it.'

'I see,' he said, his voice hard. 'Well, you seem to have given me a good deal of thought. You've got my personality neatly buttoned up, haven't you? And what about your own?'

'My—own?'

'Your personality. *Your* reasons why any relationship between us wouldn't work.'

'I don't think that has anything to do with——' Kate began, but he cut her short.

'Oh, but it surely has. It has everything to do with it. It's your personality that won't accept the chemistry between us.' He ran his hand lightly down her body, from shoulder to knee, and Kate shuddered. 'You see? If I were to kiss you now——' he bent his head nearer and she closed her eyes in an agony of desire '—you would not be able to refuse me. Shall I prove it?'

His lips were almost touching hers. With an effort that almost drained her of her last ounce of will-power, Kate twisted her head aside. 'No,' she whispered. 'No. Please. . .'

'Please? Please, what?' he taunted her. 'Please, no—or yes? Can you answer me, Kate? Do you even know?' He withdrew and looked down at her, and she was shaken to see something very like contempt in his eyes. 'Perhaps you're a tease, after all.'

'I'm not——' she began, and then stopped. Wouldn't it be better if he did think that—if he believed her to be no more than a flirt, leading him on and then eluding him? She didn't want his contempt—the thought of it hurt more deeply than she cared to admit—but it had to be better than the desire to which she could so easily—and catastrophically—succumb.

'All right,' she said, with what she hoped was a seductive flutter of her eyelashes. 'So you've called my bluff. And it was a very nice kiss. I only wish it could be more. But—as I told you—I'm really not into casual affairs. So now, if you don't mind letting me go. . .' She stood up, hearing the false note in her voice and hating it. She didn't look at him now; she couldn't.

Max moved away slightly, but he still barred her way to the door.

'Just what are you playing at, Kate?' he demanded, and his voice was like iron. 'Just what game are you playing now? I can tell you one thing—you're a damned bad actress.' With a movement so swift that she had no chance to escape, he gripped her by the shoulders, forcing her to look up at him. His eyes were blazing now, flashing blue steel that seemed as if it would cut right through into her brain, see every movement of her mind. 'What the hell's the matter with you, Kate? Can't you recognise true gold when you see it? What in heaven's name has made you so cynical? It's not the accident that killed your cousins, I'd swear to that. So what *is* it?'

He was almost shaking her now, his anger and frustration overcoming any gentleness he might have shown earlier, and Kate found herself twisting and pushing at him in a desperate effort to escape. It was too much, she thought as she thrust helplessly at the rocklike chest, pulled ineffectually at the sinewy arms. He only had to look at her for her to melt into weakness, yet he had the advantage of physical strength, too. . .Though, even at that moment, she was aware that he was not consciously using his strength against her and, although there might be bruises on her arms later, they were not deliberately inflicted. Nevertheless, he had all the advantages, and her only refuge lay in tears. And that was a device she stubbornly refused to employ.

'All right!' she shouted, driven beyond endurance by her own despairing frustration as much as by Max's angry demands. 'All right, I'll tell you why it won't work. Just let go of me, and I'll tell you. Let *go* of me,' she repeated savagely. 'I will *not* talk while you're hurting me like that. I won't!'

Max looked down at his hands, fastened around her upper arms like iron clamps. An expression of surprise crossed his face and he released his fingers, staring at them as if they were alien to him. Automatically, Kate rubbed her arms and glared up at him.

'I'm sorry,' he said with difficulty. 'I didn't intend to——'

'It's all right. It doesn't matter.' She spoke quickly, jerkily, anxious to get this over. 'Now listen to me, Max Sarsby. I don't know what sort of relationship you had in mind for us. What I do know is that it wouldn't work—whatever it is. *Nothing* would work between us, because of the kind of person you are and the kind of person I am. Yes, I admit my personality has a lot to do with it. Of course it has. And I'll tell you why.' She passed a shaking hand through her tangled hair. 'Because you frighten me. Everything about you frightens me. Your strength, your determination—and most of all, your ruthlessness. You've got a reputation for it. The "Snow Demon", who will use anyone who gets in your way as the next rung on the ladder to your own personal success. There's only one thing in your mind, and it's that trophy. You'll stop at nothing to win that. You'll trample over anyone who offers you the slightest opposition. Well, I don't want to be trampled on. I don't want to get in your way. I just want to get on with my own life, dull and dreary though it must seem to you, and cope with my own problems. And I don't want you to be one of them.'

Max stared at her. She watched his face harden as she spoke, and knew that she was getting through to him— that, somewhere, she was touching a nerve. But was it only the nerve of his arrogance, of an ego that would refuse to consider any form of criticism? Would he ever allow himself to understand what she was saying?

'Well,' he said at last, slowly, 'you really do have a low opinion of me, don't you?'

Kate shrugged. The worst of the danger was over. He

would not touch her again now. She felt relief at the thought—relief mixed, inevitably, with a deep sense of loss. 'I admire the way you've overcome your injuries, and I admire your dedication. I just think it could be put to better use. You've inspired me to overcome my own hang-ups. I think you could inspire others, too. But I don't suppose you ever will. Because you're too arrogant—too concerned with your own self-glorification. And that will repel more people than you can ever inspire.'

'And that really is how you see me?' he said quietly. 'As nothing more than a self-seeker, looking for personal glory, not caring who gets hurt so long as I make it in the end?'

Kate hesitated. She had never intended to put it as harshly as that. She looked at Max and caught again, for a brief second, that flash of vulnerability that had struck her in the restaurant on that first morning. And then it was gone. She reminded herself of what it could mean to her to become involved with him, and hardened her heart. It was better, after all, to be harsh.

'Yes,' she said simply. 'That's just how I see you.'

Max raised his eyes and looked into her face. She held his gaze, keeping her eyes steady, and, after a long moment, it was his gaze that fell away.

'Then that's all there is to be said, isn't it?' he said quietly, and turned his back on her.

CHAPTER SIX

Outside, the day had lost all its savour. It was bitterly cold; the temperature, Kate heard, was somewhere around minus twenty degrees. The little river that ran through the far end of the village was partly frozen, even though it ran fast. The trees were thick with hoar-frost and a heavy mist hung in the valley, shrouding the mountains from view. Everyone wore their thickest, warmest clothes.

Normally the cold weather didn't bother Kate. It was generally crisp, bright and dry, and you could wrap up against the low temperature. But this murky rawness seemed to eat into her bones, into her spirits, and she felt a depth of depression that she hadn't experienced for a long time. A depression she hadn't even felt when Peter and Jane had died; her grief had been sharp and clean then, an anguish that was entirely natural. This was something else, and she remembered feeling it before—over David.

It was David and the aspects of his personality that had caused her most pain that she'd recognised in Max, that had first cautioned her to be wary of him. And now, walking slowly along the road, all thoughts of skiing forgotten, she allowed the memories to flood back. Painful as they were, they might in some way help to ease this grinding misery that she now felt over Max.

Kate had been only eighteen when she first met David. She'd known about him from her father—heard all about the talented young musician who could make his violin sing so beautifully. 'He can do anything with that instrument,' John Markham had told her. 'It laughs, its cries, it practically sits up and begs. Come and hear him next week, Kate, at the rehearsal—you'll love it, I know.'

Kate had gone along to the rehearsal. It was for a symphony concert which her father would be conducting shortly at a music festival in Switzerland. Kate had enjoyed it when her father was conducting within reach of their home—too often he had been away, on long tours overseas, and although Kate and her mother had frequently gone with him, Kate had hated the disruption of their home life.

It was strange that she had taken up a travelling life herself, considering how she'd felt about home during her childhood. But dimly, Kate knew that this was only temporary. Eventually, she would find something to do that would keep her in one place. And then she would build a home—a nest in which she could retreat from the world.

Until David, she had expected to share that home with a man—a husband. But when their relationship had shattered she had turned her back on the idea of marriage. It wouldn't work—not for her. Because she found herself attracted to men of drive, of strength and power. And that invariably meant ambition.

Kate had had enough of ambition. She wanted no more of it in her life. . .

But on that first morning, sitting in the big hall listening to the rehearsal, the eighteen-year-old Kate knew nothing of this. Young, slender, wide-eyed, she slipped into a seat at the back where she might remain unnoticed, and watched as the musicians came on to the stage.

Most of them knew her, of course; as the daughter of their resident conductor, she had attended a good many of their rehearsals. A few of them noticed her sitting at the back, and gave her a wave. Kate smiled back, but made no other move, and they were all too concerned about their work to think about her for long. Casually, most of them dressed in jeans and sweaters, or other everyday clothes, they dispersed about the stage.

Kate waited. She listened as they went through the two smaller pieces which were to be played without a soloist. Her father was concentrating hard, making them go over certain parts again and again until he got just the tone and flavour he wanted. The hall echoed to the music and Kate closed her eyes, letting it wash over her.

And then David came.

To begin with, there was nothing to tell Kate that this man was going to change her life. There he was on stage, tall and fair, with straight hair that flopped on to his forehead and almost hid his bright blue eyes. He had a charming, slightly boyish smile that revealed strong white teeth, and he looked, Kate thought, like the sort of man whom elderly female concert-goers would want to take home and mother. Younger female concert-goers might have other ideas.

He stepped forward and held his violin to his chin, and the orchestra went into the first few bars of Tchaikovsky's Violin Concerto.

With the very first trembling note, Kate was lost. The music seemed to reach right through her, touching something deep inside which responded as sensitively as the strings over which David Julian was drawing his bow. The response was physically more disturbing than any sensation she had yet known; she felt it tingling through her body, along her limbs, aching into the palms of her hands and curling the soles of her feet.

Throughout the long performance—and her father did not stop the music once, but let it go right through to the end as if they were already playing to the public—Kate did not stir. She sat quite still, her eyes wide, fixed on the slight figure in the rather tattered jeans and sloppy T-shirt, who looked almost as if the violin he held were a part of him. She listened as the violin spoke to her, wept with it when it sobbed, trembled with it when it cried out the questions that could never be answered. Her mind, her spirit, her body, were all there, with every note he played; she could see the emotion in his fingers, the tension in every line of his body, and she shared it with a completeness, an abandon, that she had never known before. When the concerto ended, and the last notes throbbed away into silence, she found she was exhausted, and she sank back into her seat, too drained to move.

There was a moment of complete silence in the hall. And then the orchestra rose as one man and applauded the young violinist.

Kate watched, the tears hot in her eyes. She had never known an orchestra do such a thing before. It had been completely spontaneous, she knew that—the musicians looked as surprised as she felt. But their applause was as sincere and as appreciative as that of any audience. Kate found herself drawn to her own feet, clapping wildly with them. And as she did so, she saw David look down the hall and knew that he could see her; that even at that distance his eyes were on hers, sending messages she dared not interpret.

The applause died a little, and David turned back to the orchestra. He lifted his violin again and began to play.

The music came as a shock, and Kate sat down abruptly. She wanted to giggle at the expressions on the faces of the other musicians. Pure jazz flowed now from the violin which had sobbed so desperately only moments before. Jazz that was alternately cheerful, even raucous, and then mournfully sad—the kind of blues normally assocated with the saxophone. It was even beginning to *sound* like a saxophone, Kate thought, and she wondered at the talent—the virtuosity—that was contained in the slim figure there on the stage. He could make his career in any kind of music he liked, she realised, and later—much later—she wondered whether even at that early stage she had begun to feel a little afraid. . .

But now, thinking back, Kate knew that she'd had no premonition of any kind. She'd simply fallen in love with David, there and then—first with the look of him and with what he could do, and later with the whole man.

It had seemed unbelievable that he could have any interest in her—she was totally unmusical in that she played no instrument, could only listen, was six years younger than he—and at eighteen, that six years had seemed quite a lot—and she had been only just out of school, unsure yet just what to do with her life. And, once she'd met David, not even caring, for it all seemed so simple: her life was his, to dictate as he liked. . .

'I mean to be the best violinist the world has ever known,' he told her as they strolled in the parks that summer, taking time off between concerts. 'Sounds arrogant, I know—but I've got it, Katie, I know I have. I've been working on it since I was four years old, for goodness' sake—I ought to be able to judge what I'm capable of. And I know I haven't reached my peak yet.'

They stopped, and David flung his jacket down on the grass beside the edge of the lake. He drew Kate down beside him and they sat close together, gazing at the distant, snow-capped peaks of the mountains. This was her home, Kate thought suddenly, this beautiful country with its mountains and railways and shining cleanliness. She was English, and had been to English schools while her parents had travelled the world, but she'd always come back here to the home that they always returned to.

Yet what was a home, really? She thought of her ideal—a place where she and someone else could settle, live ordinary lives like everyone else—going out in the morning, coming home at night. A haven to rest in every day, not just once in three months as her parents sometimes did.

What sort of a home would David have?

'Good lord, I'm not going to settle down, ever!' he exclaimed, laughing. 'How could I? I'll need a base, of course—a service flat somewhere. I suppose Switzerland would be as good as anywhere else—it's pretty central, after all. But a home—with wallpaper you have to change, furniture you have to go out and choose—no, that's not my scene, Kate. You ought to understand that, with your father having travelled most of his life.' He slipped his arm around her and drew her back to lie close to him on the short, soft grass. 'I'm going to conquer the world,' he said softly. 'And you're going to be with me, Kate. Right beside me, every step of the way. . .'

Surely she had known then that it would never work? But her eyes had been too blinded by love; she had been too intoxicated with the heady sensations David's strong arms had given her, too dazed by his kisses in the sunlight and under the moon. And her life had been spent in the atmosphere of dedication to music—until then, she had known no other.

Kate still looked back on that summer as an idyll of bliss, a bliss she had never known since and never expected to know again. Whatever had happened at the end, whatever bitterness had been left in her heart, she could not deny that for a few short months she had been happy. Too happy. Nobody, she'd told herself since, over and over again, should be as happy as she'd been that summer—because the happiness David and she had shared had been taken at the cost of other people's. It had been a stolen bliss.

She hadn't known that, then. It had only become apparent to her after the festival was over, when David had extended his stay in Switzerland as a holiday— although a holiday, to David, simply meant no concerts, no rehearsals. He had still practised for a considerable part of each day, and Kate had known that this was something that would never change. There would always be more time given to his violin than to her. . .

He was living then in a tiny flat, not far from Kate's own home. He had rented it for the duration of the festival, and kept it on for another month, refusing John and Susan Markham's offer to stay with them. 'I'm a terrible guest,' he'd said disarmingly. 'I play my violin *all* the time, and I sleep odd hours, too. It's much better

for me to be on my own.' And the Markhams, used to
the ways of musicians, had understood and agreed.

. But David had been glad to use theirs as an accommodation address. His own flat had no telephone, and
he'd given John Markham's number to his agent and
others who might need to contact him quickly. And one
morning, less than a week before David was due to leave
for a concert in Berlin, Kate took a call and found it was
from his brother.

She went straight round to his flat, her face anxious.
But when David opened the door he did not seem to
notice her agitation.

'Hello, darling.' He drew her into his arms for a long
kiss. 'Mmm. You've come just in time for coffee—I've
been working since six this morning. Now aren't you
glad I'm not staying at your place?' He laughed and
released her, going over to the side-table on which a
coffee-machine was already bubbling and sending out its
delicious aroma. 'You want some, then? Never say no to
coffee, hmm?'

Kate stood still, just inside the door. 'David. I've got
some news for you. I just took a phone call and——'

'That's news? I take phone calls every day.' He was
in the frivolous mood he often was after several hours'
satisfying practice. Kate shook her head impatiently.

'No, David. Listen. It—it's bad news, I'm afraid.'

He stopped at once, his hand still poised over the jug.
'Bad news? For me?' His voice sharpened. 'The concert's
not cancelled?'

'No—no, it's nothing like that.' To her surprise, Kate
found she was speaking as if nothing could be as bad as
the concert being cancelled. She went on, trying to
imagine how she would feel on receiving similar news,

trying to soften the way she could say it, and deciding that there was no way to break it easily. 'It's your father, David,' she said quietly, and went to him, laying her hands on his shoulders. 'I'm afraid he's dead. He had a stroke and died in the night.'

David stood quite still for a moment. He closed his eyes. Then he looked down at her, searching her face.

'Dad? Dead?'

'I'm afraid so. I'm sorry, David.'

He let her go and turned back to the coffee-maker, shifting the cups about aimlessly. Kate quietly took them from him and poured the coffee.

'Sit down and drink this, David. Then I'll help you pack.'

He looked at her as if startled, but took the coffee and sat down, sipping it slowly. His eyes seemed unfocused. At last, he turned to her and looked at her as if he were seeing her for the first time.

'Did you say something about packing, Kate?'

'Yes, of course. You'll need to go home straight away, won't you? The funeral——'

'I can't go to the funeral,' he said abruptly.

Kate stared at him. 'Can't go to the funeral? But——'

'It's the concert in a few days,' he said as if speaking to a child. 'I've got to be at the concert. I can't go to England now.'

Kate stared at him. 'But this is your *father*——'

'Look, Kate, he's dead,' David said. 'What good can it do *him* if I go to his funeral? He's not going to know.'

'But what about your mother?' she cried. 'Doesn't she need to know you're there? Doesn't she need to know that you care about him—you care about *her?*'

'I'll go straight after the concert,' he said and got up to look at a chart pinned on the wall. 'Oh—no, I can't go then, there are the rehearsals for Salzburg. And then it's Tokyo—but I could probably fit in a day before going there. Or perhaps——'

'Or perhaps next Christmas, or the one after that,' Kate cut in. 'David, I don't believe this. How can you *not* want to be with your mother at a time like this? She must be heartbroken. She needs you. You can't let her down.'

'I'm not letting her down. She's got my sister with her. My younger brother. They'll look after her. Look——' he was beginning to echo Kate's impatience '—my mother knows the situation with me. My music comes first. Before anything. It always has. She won't even *expect* me to be there. She knows I can't let Berlin down. The Philharmonic—they're one of the finest orchestras in the world. I've *got* to be there.'

'And the others? Salzburg? Tokyo?'

'Those too.' He set down his cup and turned, taking her by the shoulders. 'Kate, you've got to understand this. I thought you did. My music comes before anything else. Before my family. Before my friends. Before——' He hesitated.

'Before me,' she said quietly. 'You may as well say it, David.'

'I can't say that. But—you have to understand, Kate——'

'Would you come to *my* funeral?' she broke in bitterly. 'Or would you say, "She won't know I'm there, so why bother?" Is that what you'd say, David? And our children, if anything happened to them—would you "fit them in" between planes somewhere? Would we all have to wait for you to have a few odd moments to spare for real life—or death?'

'Children?' he said blankly. 'Who ever said anything about children? I don't intend to have children, Kate. I thought you understood—I can't trail a family around the world. I need to be totally uncluttered—except for you, of course. And you won't be clutter. . .' He moved to take her in his arms, but Kate twisted away. She moved quickly out of his reach and then stood up. Her eyes were riveted on his face; it was as if she looked at a stranger.

'No, David,' she breathed, her voice seeming to come from a long way inside her. 'I won't be clutter. Because I won't be there.' She shook her head slowly, unbelievingly. 'You know, you still don't seem to have taken this in. Your father's just died. Back in England, your family's going through hell. They're having to come to terms with sudden death. Your mother's facing life as a widow. All right, she's got your sister and your brother with her—but they're both younger than you. They all need your support. And you're just refusing to give it. You don't even seem to feel any grief. I think you've forgotten it already!'

David bowed his head. 'I haven't forgotten it, Kate. I'm not totally callous. But my parents gave up a lot to get me where I am. Dropping it now would be letting them down—my mother understands that. I told you, she won't even expect me to go home. I'll ring her in a minute—talk to her—you'll see.'

'I'll see nothing of the sort,' Kate said tonelessly. 'I'm sorry, David. You may be right—but I just can't believe it. Whatever you think, I *know* your mother would like you with her now. And missing Berlin wouldn't ruin

your career. Everyone has to miss a concert sometimes.
No—you just don't want to miss the opportunity, do
you? The opportunity of impressing even more people
with your genius. Because that's why you play, David.
Not because music means so much to you—but because
you mean so much to yourself. It's nothing more than
showing off. You love it. You love the applause. And
you won't do without it—not even to be beside your
mother at your father's funeral.' Contempt seared
through her voice and blazed from her eyes. 'Go and
ring your mother now, David—it's the very least you
can do. But I shan't be around to hear what she says.
I'm leaving now—and I won't be coming back!'

'Oh, Kate, don't be so childish!' he snapped in
exasperation. 'Of course you'll be back. We're going out
to dinner tonight, remember? And we're making plans
for our future.' He held out his arms and tilted his head
to one side, smiling the boyish smile that had always
caught at her heart. 'Our future together.'

Kate looked at him steadily. The boyish smile had no
effect on her now, except to make her see that he really
was still a boy—and perhaps always would be. A spoilt
child, whose undoubted genius with a violin had saved
him the trouble of ever having to grow up.

'No, David,' she said quietly. 'We won't be making
any plans. I don't want the kind of future you offer me.
It's no future at all. It's a vacuum—a sterile space which
you'll carry round the world with you, containing only
me and your music. No family—no friends—just concert
after concert, with you feeding off the applause and
nothing for me.' She shook her head. 'I don't think you'll
ever find a woman who wants that kind of life, David.'

His face hardened and his arms dropped. He gave her

one last, long look, with eyes that had suddenly turned
to ice. And then he shrugged and turned away, and she
saw that his hands were already reaching out for the
violin that lay across a small table.

'Ring your mother, David,' she said, and slipped
quietly through the door. . .

It had taken Kate a long time to recover from David.
Her parents had said little, but she knew that they
understood and grieved for her. She had turned back to
them for a while, afraid to venture again into life, and
slowly they had encouraged her to become independent.
It had been her father's idea that she work as a holiday
rep—with her languages and her knowledge of Europe,
and especially of the mountain areas where they had
spent so many happy times walking in summer and
skiing in winter, it would be a job she could handle
easily, and one which would develop her self-reliance.
And she had needed every ounce of that self-reliance in
the early days.

She needed it again now, she thought. Why did she
have to fall in love all over again with a man of ambition?
Although Max Sarsby was a different man entirely from
David—no spoilt child here, he was a fully mature man
of considerable strength, both physical and emotional.
She had felt that strength from the moment they had
met, and had feared it, knowing that it could be more
than she could resist. And so it had almost proved.

In a way, that brief relationship with David had been
a good thing. It had prepared her for the much more
powerful dangers Max had presented. Without the
experience of David behind her, she might well have
succumbed to Max's charms—might well have gone

with him, blindly, into a future that could only have been disaster.

Suddenly, she wished that she could be flying back to England with the current batch of guests. Then she need never see Max again.

CHAPTER SEVEN

WITH February came the busiest time in all the ski resorts. The Continental holiday coincided with the British half-term, and skiers poured into the village, filling the hotels and *Gasthäuser* and forming long queues at all the lifts. Fortunately, there were enough lifts and runs for a good dispersal once on the mountain, and sufficient restaurants to cope with the crowds. All the same, Kate thought she preferred the quieter times, and she was thankful that her company did not run any weeks during that period solely for beginners. Skiers with only a few days' tuition were likely to be nervous enough the first time they were taken away from the village nursery slopes and up on the mountain; the crowds of experienced skiers now flashing down the runs would have terrified them.

She and Max had little contact. He seemed to have taken her at her word and dismissed any idea that there could be any kind of relationship between them. In the house, when they inevitably met, he was polite—too polite. His eyes were cold and hard, like points of steel, when he looked at her, and she felt the sharp chill right into her heart. She had to remind herself, when the weight of misery threatened to become too much, that this was what she had wanted—that Max Sarsby could be no good to her, could bring only heartbreak. But it was difficult to accept when she knew her body was crying out for him, craving his touch; when she lay awake at night yearning for his kisses; when she dreamed of him in her fitful sleep—dreamed that they were together at last, and woke to the cruel reality that he could never be hers.

Why did I have to fall in love with him? she asked herself miserably. Why did he have to come here? But there was no answer to her despairing questions.

Angrily, she shook herself. What sort of a woman was she, anyway, hankering after a man her own common sense had told her was bad news? Didn't she have any control over this ridiculous yearning? Couldn't she simply tell herself that it was all for the best, that she'd done the right thing? That she'd forget him anyway as soon as he left the village, and she no longer risked meeting him on any street corner, in any restaurant, on the *pistes*, or even on the stairs outside her own room?

Of course she could! And the fact that he was now seeing even more of the tall and statuesque Helga ought to be a help.

Kate sometimes wondered how Helga managed to have so much free time to spend with Max. They seemed to be everywhere together. On her own days off, she would see them up on the mountain, skiing the black runs or disappearing off-*piste* to ski in powder snow, clean and unmarked by the trails of other skiers. Late in the afternoons, when the skiers were gathering in bars and restaurants for drinks and snacks and laughter, she would see them again, cosily close in some dim corner, a jug of *glühwein* between them, or sipping mugs of hot chocolate topped with foaming cream. And at night, when the stars hung like a heavy frost in the velvet sky, she would see them walking slowly, arms entwined, along the village street, or catch a glimpse of them clattering past in one of the horse-drawn sleighs that could be hired to visit distant inns.

It was true that Helga had more free time than most of the ski instructors. She had now stopped taking classes, and gave private tuition to those who were willing to pay more for a couple of hours, or perhaps a day, with an instructor who would give them full attention. And she was a good instructor—Kate had to give her that. Added to the glamour of her sun-tanned face, her blue eyes and chestnut hair, she possessed an easy manner and apparently unlimited patience. Those who paid for Helga's time and expertise invariably considered it money well spent.

'Really, she is wasted here,' one of the other instructors, Klaus, observed to Kate. 'She could work in one of the big resorts—Kitzbühel or Wengen. In fact, I have never really understood why Helga didn't go in for competition skiing.'

'She's that good?' Kate looked across the bar in which they were sitting, to where Helga was laughing with a group of her pupils. For once, Max wasn't around. He was probably still up on the mountain somewhere, doing one of the gruelling runs he had evolved as part of his training programme.

'Oh, she's good.' Klaus followed her glance, his own full of admiration. 'There are a lot of things Helga could have done, I think—skiing, skating, modelling. I would never have been surprised if she had gone into films or TV—you must admit she has the appearance for it.'

'Oh, she certainly has that.' Helga could have taken part in one of the big American soaps any day of the week, Kate thought, and tried to imagine her effect if she were to appear in *Dallas* or *Dynasty*. 'So why does she stay here, in such a small village?'

Klaus shrugged. 'That, nobody knows. I am sure she has her reasons—but, being Helga, she does not discuss them.'

Kate knew what he meant. There was something unapproachable about Helga, for all her apparently extrovert qualities. She had an arrogance that was almost royal. If she decided to keep her reasons for staying in the village private, there would be few who would dare to question her.

'Anyway,' Klaus said, turning back to Kate, his brown eyes warm and smiling, 'why are we discussing Helga? I wanted to talk about us. Where have you been all my life, Kate?'

Kate gave him a teasing grin. 'Now then, Klaus. You needn't pretend you've been languishing for want of my company—I've seen you, chatting up a new pupil every week. And always the prettiest, I've noticed! What's the matter—isn't there anyone in this class that takes your fancy?'

Klaus looked hurt. 'Chatting up? I don't understand. And what is this *fancy* you speak of? You know how bad my English is, Kate.'

'Your English is very nearly as good as mine,' she told him. 'And if you don't know what those phrases mean, I'm sure you can work it out. . .Klaus, I didn't just fall off a Christmas tree, you know. I've been a ski rep for three years now—I know just what you instructors are like. A new girl every week, unless you're already attached. It's like a competition between you!'

'Now, Kate, that isn't fair,' he protested. 'Look at me—am I not a good, clean-living Austrian? Do I *want* trouble? That's what those who live as you suggest end up with, you know. And there are too many kinds of trouble, too. No, it's not for me. Chatting up, yes, perhaps. It is expected. But more than that—no. Not for someone who is here only for a week or two. Now, you, Kate, are here for much longer than that. . .' He reached out and took her hand. Kate looked at him, doubtful, but still laughing at his pleading, spaniel-like expression. And at that moment the door opened and Max walked in.

He saw her immediately. She saw his eyes on her laughing face. And then his glance dropped to the table, where her hand lay clasped in Klaus's.

Max turned abruptly. For a moment Kate thought he was going to walk out. Then Helga's clear voice hailed him from her table and he marched over to her. He did not give Kate another glance.

It was over in seconds, yet in that time she felt a tumult of emotions, a rush of warring feelings that blinded and confused her. She wanted desperately to explain—to tell him that she and Klaus were merely teasing, having a little fun. But hard on the heels of that thought came another—what would it matter to him, after all? Hadn't he made it clear that he had discarded any idea of a relationship with her, that he had turned quite positively to Helga? And, following that thought, a third—that, in any case, it was better that he should think her involved with Klaus. That it couldn't be a bad thing at all. . .

She lifted her eyes to Klaus's face and smiled. 'So I'm fair game, am I, simply because I'll be here for a bit longer?' she said challengingly. 'Klaus, you're incorrigible! You really do think we're all just dying to fall in love with the handsome ski instructors, don't you? You think you just have to crook your little finger and we'll all come running—skiers, reps, holiday-makers, all of us.'

'Well, of course,' Klaus said, looking injured. 'Because it's true.' And as Kate burst out laughing, he smiled, too. 'Look around you, Kate, at all the young girls there are here. Some of them have their boyfriends with them, and they're happy enough. But many others come alone, or with another girl. They want only to find a man to keep them company for a week—to laugh with, to flirt a little, to add that certain spice to their holiday. It's no more than that for most. And it's fun for us all. Instructing can become a little the same, you know, when you are doing it all the time.'

'So why don't you stick to the girls in your class?' Kate asked. 'As you say, it's fun, and you don't run into any danger. Why take the risk of choosing a rep, who's staying in the village for months and could become a problem?'

Klaus looked at her and she saw with a slight shock that his dark eyes were serious now, their laughter gone, the teasing disappeared.

'I have wondered that myself,' he said quietly.

Kate bit her lip. She hadn't expected to get into deep water with Klaus, and she didn't want it. He was a nice enough boy—but that, she thought, was how she regarded him. As a boy. Probably, he was the same age as herself, about twenty-four. But he seemed a decade younger in experience—he had lived all his life in this one small village, had probably had no more than two or three love affairs, and none of them very serious. His past contained none of the tragedies and heartache that her own life had suffered.

Recognising that it was already too late, she tried to change the subject.

'Are you looking forward to the village race next Saturday?' she asked cheerfully. 'I am. I've heard it's great fun. Do you enter?'

'Oh, yes, all the instructors enter. And everyone in the village who skis.' His young face lit up and he smiled at her, his white teeth flashing in his tanned face. 'Of course, you don't know who your partner will be—it might be someone old or someone young. If you are very lucky, it might be someone you especially admire. Nearly every year the race brings at least one romance—and often a marriage to follow.' There was a sly look in his eyes now, as he glanced up at her from beneath long dark lashes. 'Perhaps it will be so this year. I wonder who will be the lucky one?'

Well, if it's not you this year, it certainly will be before long, Kate thought. Those dark brown eyes, and the way you use them—not to mention that nice, strong body. . . She felt a momentary regret that she could not respond to Klaus's charms herself. Surely he would be just the kind of partner for her? Cheerful, uncomplicated, easy to live with, and clearly extremely virile. What more could any girl ask?

Nothing—if you were actually *looking* for a partner. But she wasn't, was she? She'd decided long ago that a single life was a great deal easier to manage. She liked her freedom, and she'd made up her mind to keep it.

So why did her eyes stray to that far corner, which the other skiers had now left empty. . .except for Max and Helga? Why did she look at their heads, the one so dark, the other so tawny, close enough for their hair to emerge and twine together, as she so often imagined them entwined at night in some dark and quiet room. . .and why did she feel this cold hand closing round her heart, chilling and freezing it within her?

Determinedly, she turned back to Klaus and gave his hand a sudden squeeze.

'Perhaps we'll be partners on Sunday,' she said with a deliberate note of optimism in her voice. 'That would be fun, wouldn't it? I'd like to ski the race with you, Klaus.'

But, as she might have foreseen, things turned out quite differently.

The racers gathered together at the foot of the nursery slopes early on Saturday morning. Kate was there with the rest of them, looking forward to the day's fun which would make a welcome change from the routine of her life. Fortunately all her guests changed on Sundays— that was her busiest day, when she had to be up early to see guests off, travel with the coaches to Salzburg, see that everyone went satisfactorily through the check-in and Customs, await the flights that brought the new influx of skiers and travel back with them. Often, she would have to be up by five a.m. And, if there were any delays or hitches, might not see her bed again until after midnight. And there would be no sleeping-in on Monday, either—that was the day when she needed to be down at the nursery slopes, looking after her guests and making sure that all the lift-passes and vouchers were in order.

Saturday was relatively quiet. And with almost everyone either taking part in the race or watching it, Kate was free to enjoy the day with the rest of them.

This was not, of course, the weekly race which the ski-school organised. That took place each Friday, with the people who had attended classes that week thronging the hillside at various points to begin their own class races—the beginners lowest on the slope, the intermediates a little higher, and the advanced skiers at the very top, lining the ridge by the summit of the T-bar lift.

Today's was an annual race, a tradition begun when the lift had been first installed and the first *piste* made smooth. It was open to all, but, although many visitors took part, it was unmistakably a local event, and there was much laughter and teasing as men and women Kate had never seen on skis jostled each other to sign their names and qualify for the draw, when each name would be taken separately—one from the hat containing men's tickets and one from the bonnet containing women's. Even the Brunners were there, she saw, and young Dieter's face was aflame with excitement. He was holding the hand of a young village girl, both clearly hoping to be drawn to race together. Kate smiled and wondered if they would be one of this year's romances. 'I see you've decided to take part in the festivities,' a voice drawled at her side, and she turned to find Max and Helga beside her.

'Why not? It's fun—an obstacle race on skis. I was in one a couple of years ago at another village—I drew the oldest man there, I think!'

'Let's hope you'll be luckier this time,' Max observed, and Kate, following his glance, saw Klaus making his way through the crowd towards her.

'And are you taking part, or have you just come to watch?' she enquired politely, dividing her question between Max and Helga. The German girl answered her, her voice as cool as always, a smile on her golden face.

'Oh, Max and I will take part, of course—won't we, *liebling*? Perhaps we may even be drawn to ski together.' The look on her face left Kate in no doubt that they would be—clearly, the chief ski instructor had already been primed as to his duty. 'We make a good team, do we not, Max?'

'A very good team,' he answered, smiling down at her, and Kate turned away, fighting down a sick jealousy. Angrily, she scolded herself for being unreasonable. You don't want him—why not let Helga have him? She can cope with his ambition, since she almost certainly shares it herself. She'll help him every inch of the way towards that coveted trophy. She's *right* for him.

Klaus was at her side now, touching her arm to gain her attention, and she turned to him with some relief. His doglike devotion was certainly soothing, and she was fairly sure it didn't go too deeply. Klaus was young yet—he wasn't really in love with her, just playing with the idea, and once she left the village at the beginning of April, when the snow began to melt, he would quickly forget her.

'They're starting the draw,' Klaus murmured as the crowd fell silent, and Kate turned towards the small podium on which the chief instructor had taken up his position.

He spoke rapidly for a few moments, explaining the race for the benefit of the visitors, and welcoming all the participants. Later on, he told them, there would be a torchlight skiing display, when the instructors would ski in formation, each holding a blazing torch, and there would be a barbecue and a fondue party, with free drinks, for everyone who had taken part in the race. Today was the day when the village celebrated—a party day, when the only requirement made was that all should be happy.

'Happy,' Kate heard Max murmur, close beside her. 'Are *you* happy, Kate?' But she pretended not to have heard him.

The chief instructor began to draw the names. Each pair produced some reaction—an 'ooh' or 'ah' filled with meaning from the villagers at some combinations, a roar of laughter at others; shouts and ribald comments from the holiday skiers as their own companions were drawn to ski, either with each other or a local man or woman.

Klaus, to his obvious disappointment, was drawn to ski with a middle-aged village woman. 'My aunt,' he whispered to Kate, and she gave him a smile of commiseration. His aunt looked a very nice woman, but she could see that, for Klaus, half the fun of the race had already disappeared.

Helga, looking equally chagrined, drew one of the other instructors. A good match, Kate thought, glancing across at the handsome young man she had seen so often on the slopes. A pity this couldn't be one of those combinations which led to romance... And then she jerked back to attention as she heard her own name called.

A cheer was going up from the crowd. She stared about her, dazed.

'Who is it?' she asked, turning first to Klaus, and then to Max. 'Why are they cheering like that? Who am I to ski with?'

'It couldn't have been better planned,' Max answered, his eyes alight and vibrant. 'I don't think anyone will ever again believe that the whole thing isn't a put-up job. You're skiing with me, Kate—that's why they're cheering. They obviously think we're a good match.' His eyes were on her, disturbingly intent. 'Can several hundred skiers be wrong?' he asked softly, and her heart kicked. 'Maybe this really is what they say—a magic day, when futures are determined and lives changed. What do you say, Kate? Do you dare to ski with me—or would you rather withdraw now?'

Kate looked back at him. She kept her own eyes cool and steady, returning his look without any hint of the emotions churning inside. Did it really have to happen this way? she asked silently. Don't I have enough problems with this man, without this? But she was determined not to let him see any hint of what her real feelings might be.

'Withdraw?' she echoed. 'Why ever should I want to do that? Of course we'll ski together, Max. Let's show them all what English skiers can do, shall we? You never know—we might even win.'

'We might indeed,' he agreed gravely, and his eyes were once more disconcertingly intent. 'And as you know, nothing less than winning satisfies me—whatever the competition might be.'

Kate stared at him. She felt a tiny shiver run down her spine. Just what did he mean by that last remark? For it wasn't just skiing he was talking about, she was sure. What else did he hope—mean—to win? And what could it possibly mean to her?

She had tried to convince herself that Max Sarsby was no longer interested in her and the 'chemistry'—or whatever it was—that existed between them. Now she was no longer sure. And the thought filled her heart with foreboding.

Nevertheless, she came down the last twisting run to the foot of the nursery slope laughing, her eyes alight and her face glowing. Her hand was clasped firmly in Max's as they came through the last few slalom gates, her arm pressed close against his, and when she looked up and met his eyes she saw an answering laughter there, and felt warmed by the simple pleasure they had both so unexpectedly experienced in this village race.

It was quite different from the usual kind of skiing race. The course, starting at the top of the hill, was scattered with obstacles, all of which must be negotiated on skis. It demanded a fairly high degree of skill, and there was no chance of cheating—each obstacle was watched over by checkers, who were as strict as they were good-humoured.

Max and Kate had waited their turn, and then rode up the T-bar together. As always, Kate was burningly conscious of his arm, pressed close against hers as they rose slowly up the slope. She wished that she could lean away from him, but knew that to do so would inevitably result in them both falling off—a fate which could not even be contemplated. Though it would certainly serve the purpose of getting them out of the race, she thought, momentarily tempted—and concentrated fiercely on keeping her skis parallel.

'Here we go, then,' Max said when they had glided off the T-bar and were waiting at the start. 'That's the first obstacle—down there. A narrow run between two fences. And we'll have to ski close, one behind the other.

Suppose I go first and you put your arms round my waist?'

Kate nodded. It was what the other skiers would have done, and she had no intention of treating Max any differently from any other partner. She slid into position, wrapped her arms firmly around Max's waist and waited for the signal to start.

They glided easily down the slope. Kate had skied in tandem before many times—but never quite like this. It was almost as if their bodies had become one; she seemed to know exactly when Max intended to make a turn, exactly what weight to apply. They reached the traverse between the fences and held a steady course before making the final turn that brought them out of it; then they separated, skiing side by side down to the next obstacle.

This was a pile of clothing which they had to put on as best they could, in constant danger of skidding away down the hill as they arrayed themselves in an assortment of shawls, bonnets and masks. Each skier had not only to wear the clothes, but also an animal 'head'. Kate found herself pulling on the long ears and whiskers of a rabbit, while Max was almost frightening in the black and gold stripes of a tiger. They looked at each other for a moment.

Kate felt a tremor run through her body. Was it really coincidence that they should have been given these particular masks? Looking at Max now, she could almost believe in him as a tiger—a tiger in the snow, dangerous and predatory. She felt a stab of panic. What was she doing with him, up here on this lonely mountainside, anyway? She felt herself shrink away from the glittering eyes.

'Come on,' Max said, his voice oddly rough inside the mask. 'We're losing time.'

They swept on down the slope, negotiating each obstacle as they came to it, and gradually Kate relaxed. Max was clearly taking the race in the spirit in which it was intended—as nothing more than fun. Everyone in the village knew by now who he was, and accepted his presence; nobody stared at him or gossiped about him, and he seemed generally well-liked. And now here he was, joining in their own race, and they were prepared to cheer him every inch of the way.

The last obstacle was a gate. They had to ski through it, separately, the man first. Before he allowed his partner through, he was expected to exact a kiss.

Kate hesitated. The gate was in clear view of everyone watching. She looked at Max, mute appeal in her eyes.

'You can't,' she said, 'not with these awful masks on.'

'That,' Max said, 'is easily remedied.' And he whipped off her rabbit's head and dropped it in the snow. His own tiger's mask followed quickly, and, positioning himself so that his skis did not slip, he leaned over the gate and took her into his arms.

Kate had expected a brief peck, the kind that the other skiers had given their partners before skiing down to the finish as quickly as possible to make good time. But Max seemed to have forgotten about the race— forgotten, for once, about winning. He held her close and set his mouth firmly against hers. And Kate, helpless in the snow, could do nothing. Nothing, except respond.

Even here—with so many people watching—her treacherous body gave her away. Even here, half leaning over a flimsy gate, her skis scrabbling desperately for a secure hold, with the cheers and calls of the crowd roaring in her ears, she still responded—still felt that fire lick through her, the flames of desire lighting in her heart, her stomach, her mind. She tried to shake her head, tried to deny what was happening to her, but could not. And it was with a mixture of relief and dismay that she felt her skis finally slide uncontrollably away, so that she fell heavily against Max's straining body and they both collapsed in a tangled heap of skis, legs, arms and brightly coloured shawls.

They picked themselves up with some difficulty, half laughing, half shaken by the force of desire which had taken them both by surprise. Kate was up first—she dared not give Max the chance to take her hand again, even to pull her to her feet. She waited a moment until he was on his feet, too, and then, not waiting to brush the snow from their suits, they took off again and skied down to the finish.

'I don't think we'll have won, somehow,' Max murmured in her ear as they came to a halt, 'but it was worth it.' And there was a glint in his eye that told Kate he was laughing at her—that he'd probably intended it to happen from the start. And, although her mind told her to be indignant, instinct would only allow her to smile back at him, still dazed by the impact of their kiss.

Hand in hand, they glided over to the ring of faces lining the temporary fence. Many of Kate's guests were there, and they all congratulated her loudly, reaching over to clap her on the back. Helga was there, too, having completed her run earlier; her eyes were fixed on Max, and she barely acknowledged Kate.

'At last! I thought you were never coming down,' she complained. 'What happened?' Her eyes were full of suspicion as she looked from one to the other, and Kate laughed.

'I thought our time was quite good, didn't you, Max? Except at the gate, perhaps. . .' She laughed again at Helga's expression, and then turned deliberately away from them both to link arms with Klaus, who had just appeared at her side. 'Klaus, what I need most of all right now is *eine grosse schokolade*. Let's go and track one down, shall we?'

'Just a minute,' Max called as they began to move away. 'Why don't we all meet up at the fondue party later on? It should be fun, and I've got an idea we're supposed to stick with our partners for the rest of the day, aren't we?'

'I've never heard that——' Klaus began doubtfully, but he was interrupted by Helga, whose face was flushed with what looked very like irritation—even temper.

'Nonsense, Max, my darling! There is no such rule. And, in any case, Klaus and I were not partners—he skied with his aunt, didn't you, Klaus?'

'With whom you certainly couldn't expect him to spend the rest of the day,' Max said smoothly. 'So let's consider it settled, shall we? We'll meet back here for the torchlight skiing—you'll be taking part in that, anyway, both of you—and then go on to the fondue party together. And now, I think Kate's idea is the best I've heard all day. A large hot chocolate and one of those delicious pastries—just what's wanted after an energetic morning's skiing.'

Kate turned her head and found Helga staring at her. There was a mixture of rage and bafflement in the German girl's eyes, and for once Kate felt in complete sympathy with her. It's not my fault, she said silently. *I* don't want to do it, either. But she knew it was no use saying so.

Klaus, like every other young man in the village, would jump at the chance of spending time with one of the great downhill skiers. And Max. . .

Max had won again. As he intended to do. Always.

CHAPTER EIGHT

THE afternoon was devoted to races and games for the children and less advanced skiers—though most of the local children could ski almost as soon as they could walk. Kate was always amused by the amazement of the holiday skiers—particularly the beginners—at the prowess of quite small children. 'Three years old at the outside!' she'd heard one man say, quite indignantly. 'And coming straight down the hill at about forty miles an hour, with *no poles*! And as for those kids who get on the lifts after school—they're straight over the edge, you know, and down while I'm still getting my poles sorted out.'

'And they've never heard of queues,' someone else chimed in. 'Half a dozen of them were here yesterday—only about eight or nine years old—and they were all round me, getting in front and on the T-bar, and do you know, the same lot were up and down and getting in front of me *again*, before I'd even been up once.'

'I don't let them get away with it any more,' contributed a sour-faced man who was on his first skiing holiday, but had evidently read all the books, and talked with what Kate suspected was a purely theoretical knowledge about stem turns and uphill christies and *wedelning*. 'I put my pole in between the tips of their skis. That stops them. Cheeky little so-and-so's!'

Kate smiled, but did not add to the conversation. She heard it every week from skiers who were half awed, half irritated by the antics of the local children who were so maddeningly adept—and knew it. I suppose I was one myself once, she reflected, thinking back to the days when she, too, had been taken out on the slopes on a pair of tiny skis and taught to *schuss* and turn in the soft snow. She certainly felt a good deal of sympathy for the local youngsters, who took a not unnaturally proprietory attitude towards their village slopes and could hardly wait for school to finish early every afternoon, so that they could get out and use the lift-passes that had been their main Christmas presents.

This afternoon, she watched with pleasure as they showed off their skill in their own races. For a short time, she was alone—Max had decided to go up for an afternoon on one of the black runs, working on his technique as he did every day. Helga had disappeared without explanation, and Klaus had gone home to prepare for the torchlight procession in which he, along with the other ski instructors and some of the advanced skiers, was taking part.

'You should come too, Kate,' he'd urged her, but Kate had shaken her head. Skiing in the darkness carrying a blazing torch was fun—she'd done it before several times—but watching was even better. And when darkness fell that evening, she was in position early, determined to get a good view.

'Quite a romantic scene,' a voice drawled in her ear, and she jumped a little.

'You had a good afternoon?' she asked coolly, without turning her head. She might have known Max would find her here. Perhaps she had known? And if so, she thought in exasperation, why had she chosen just this spot to stand? Wouldn't she have been better to find some other place—a corner where nobody would look?

But then Klaus wouldn't have found her, either. And after the procession was over she had a date with Klaus, at the fondue party. The date was with Max—and Helga—as well. But Klaus was her buffer, her protection.

Anyway, what could possibly happen here, in the middle of the crowd watching the procession? Even Max Sarsby couldn't present any threat to her here—could he?

'You're looking extremely glamorous tonight,' the velvety voice went on. 'Is that a new jacket?'

'Not particularly.' After all, she'd had it for at least a week. . . She felt ridiculously pleased that he'd noticed it, though. She turned her head, brushing back her shimmering hair with one hand to let the blonde strands cascade over the glowing red of her ski-jacket. Beneath it, she wore a black velvet neck-piece over a tight-fitting black sweater and trousers. Her only jewellery was a thin gold chain round her neck, a present from her parents on her twenty-first birthday, matching the narrow strap of her wrist-watch. For make-up she wore only a green eyeliner which made her eyes look even wider than usual, and a lipstick that echoed the colour of her jacket; the golden tan of her smooth skin needed no further enhancement.

With a slight shock, she saw that Max, too, appeared different tonight—dangerous, menacing, bringing back thoughts of the tiger whose mask he had worn during the race. He stood very close—closer than she liked— and seemed to loom over her, so that she had to lean back slightly to look up at him. And he, too, was wearing black—a skin-tight racing suit that outlined his body in all its virile muscularity. Its darkness was relieved only by a diagonal red slash that ran from shoulder to hip. Above it, his teeth and eyes gleamed as he smiled at her, but to Kate it was the smile of a predator, watching his prey, anticipating the pleasures to come. . .

Instinctively, she stepped back.

'Isn't Helga with you?' At that moment, she would have welcomed the presence of the German girl—Max Sarsby was altogether too close, altogether too magnetic.

'She's in the procession.' The teeth gleamed again. 'So we can watch together—just you and I.'

'Well, you and I and several hundred others,' Kate said with a half-hearted attempt at a joke, but Max shook his head.

'No. Just you and I. I've found a vantage-point, where we can be nice and private. Come with me.'

'But I'm quite happy——' Kate's words were jerked from her throat as Max's fingers closed firmly round her waist and drew her away. Taking a deep breath, she opened her mouth to protest loudly, and then caught the interested glances of some of the bystanders and closed it again. No gossip, Max had said during their first encounter, and she knew enough about him now to know that he'd appeared in more than one gossip column in the past—and would again, if his return to skiing was successful. Max Sarsby had been famous for his prowess with women as well as on the ski slopes—and Kate had no desire to appear in the newspapers as his latest conquest. Particularly as her name, as daughter of the famous conductor John Markham, would itself attract interest.

Max shifted his grip so that he was holding her hand,

keeping it in a close, warm clasp that Kate knew she would be quite unable to break. Cursing him silently, she walked by his side through the narrow streets, now thronged with people hurrying to the best view-points of the slopes. Where could Max be taking her? What vantage-point did he know of that wasn't likely to be known to a hundred others? Well, at least they wouldn't be alone—at least she'd have the protection of the other watchers.

But as Max turned into the side door of one of the hotels, Kate wasn't so sure.

'Where are you taking me? I don't want——' But again her words were interrupted, this time by Max's free hand, which he placed over her mouth. Furious, she struggled against him, but her own strength seemed to evaporate as he lifted her easily against him and half carried her up the stairs. At the top, he set her on her feet again and looked down into her angry green eyes.

'Well, will you be quiet, Kate? Or do I have to gag you?'

'You don't have to do anything but let me go!' she hissed. 'Where are you taking me? How *dare* you? I demand you let me go at once!'

He laughed softly. 'Not yet, my Kate. Don't you want to see the procession? I'm merely ensuring that you can. You won't get a better view from anywhere than from here, I promise you. Now. . .quietly. I happen to know that there's a newspaper correspondent staying in this hotel, and you wouldn't want to feature in the racier gossip columns, would you?'

Kate bit her lip and followed him, her hand still firmly held in his, along the corridor to the door at the end. Max paused, felt in his pocket and took out a key.

'Soon be there now,' he murmured cheerfully, and unlocked the door.

It had to be a bedroom, of course; she'd known that the moment he brought her into the hotel. But she was surprised to find it such a large, sumptuous one.

Max let her go. He locked the door on the inside and slipped the key back into his pocket. Then he leaned back and smiled at her.

'And now,' Kate said dangerously, 'perhaps you'll tell me what this is all about.'

Max shrugged. 'About? Why, I've already told you that. You wanted to see the procession.' He stepped across to the window, a huge pane of glass stretching from floor to ceiling. 'Look.'

Reluctantly, Kate crossed the room and stood beside him.

'Will you get a better view than that from anywhere?' Max demanded.

'Probably not,' Kate conceded, looking out at the slopes that rose immediately in front of her, white and shining in the light of the full moon that had just risen on the other side of the valley. From here, she could see, too, the narrower trails that ran between the trees and formed part of the *piste*, used when beginners were gaining in confidence. The lift rose on her left, and the whole slope was bounded by the inky darkness of close-packed pines.

'They should be starting any minute,' Max said softly in her ear. 'Why don't we make ourselves comfortable?'

Before Kate could speak, he had turned and pulled a large, white-covered couch into position in front of the big window. He touched a switch and the lights went out, dimming the room so that it was lit by no more than the glow of the street-lights and the reflected glimmer of the snow. Then he came and stood beside Kate again.

'Why don't you take your jacket off, Kate? And sit down.' He quirked a smile at her. 'I really have gone to quite a lot of trouble to get this view-point for you, you know—and I'd like you to enjoy it in comfort.'

Kate gave him a look of extreme doubt. Just why *had* he gone to so much trouble? Had he been expecting to share it with Helga? Perhaps he hadn't realised that the other girl would be expected to ski in the procession. And why had he brought her here the way he had, almost by force—and locking the door, too, so that she couldn't escape. Escape—the word made her shiver. As if she were his prisoner—which, she thought with a sudden sinking of her heart, she surely was.

Max was still standing in front of her, his hands held out.

'I'll take your jacket, shall I? You must take it off, Kate—you'll get hot.'

'And then I won't feel the benefit of it when I go out again,' she quipped, quoting from childhood days. Well, it was true enough. Slowly, she unzipped the thickly padded garment and slipped out of it. Max took it and hung it over a nearby chair, and Kate sat down, her black-clad figure a slender shadow on the white couch.

Max put his hands to his throat and began to pull down his own zip, and Kate eyed him warily. That suit was skin-tight—he surely couldn't be wearing anything beneath it? Her fears grew as she caught sight of the dark hairs curling on his chest, and her heart skipped. Max caught her eye and grinned, and Kate turned hastily away. She heard the sound of the zip again, then felt him drop down beside her on the couch. Slowly, she turned to look at him.

'It's all right,' Max said, a quiver of laughter in his voice. 'I don't intend to frighten the horses. Not just yet, anyway.'

Relief brought a sharp note to Kate's voice. 'I still don't know how you arranged this place—or why! We could have watched perfectly well from outside.'

'Why sit in the stalls when you can have a box?' he said lazily, and stretched his body beside her. Kate glanced at him again, under her lashes, unable to prevent her eyes from dwelling on the broad chest, the swelling muscles and shadowy hairs. The zip was unfastened to mid-chest; the tautness of the material drew the suit equally tightly back, leaving a deep V that she wanted, almost uncontrollably, to stroke.

'You still haven't told me how you managed it,' she reminded him tartly.

Max slanted a look at her from quizzical blue eyes.

'Relax, Kate. You're a bundle of nerves tonight. Why does it matter so much, anyway?' He smiled that devasatating smile—oh, why did he have to be so damned *attractive*?—and then sat up a little. 'All right, if it'll make you any happier. It just so happens that a friend of mine was coming to stay here. He was supposed to be arriving yesterday, but he got delayed. He can't come, after all, so he offered me the use of his room for the week. Satisfied?'

Kate watched him narrowly. 'Not really. It sounds decidedly thin to me. Who is this friend?'

'What difference does that make to you? You won't know his name. Look, I'm sorry, Kate, but you'll have to either believe me or not believe me, take your choice.

I shan't be using the room—I'm quite comfortable enough at the Brunners'—but it just struck me that it would be a marvellous place to watch the procession from. I knew you wouldn't come with me without a lot of arguing and explaining, so I dragged you more or less by force. I've got a feeling that's the only way you'll ever be persuaded to do *anything*—by being dragged into it. For the first time in my life, I find myself in sympathy with cavemen!' He stopped and looked at her with exasperation. 'Now, you can either go or stay—take your pick. But *I'm* staying, because I want to see this procession. And afterwards I shall go to the fondue party, as arranged. You. . .' he flicked something at her; it dropped to the floor and Kate, bending to pick it up, discovered that it was the key to the room '. . .can do as you like. All right?'

Kate looked at the key. She looked at Max and tried to analyse the expression on his shadowed face, but the room was too dim. She felt suddenly ashamed.

'All right,' she said in a small voice, giving the key back to him. 'I'll stay—if you don't mind. I—I'd like to.'

For a moment, Max didn't move. Then he turned his head and smiled at her, and Kate felt her bones begin to melt.

'Mind?' he said, and his voice was deep and warm and smooth. 'Come here, you obstinate little minx.' Shyly, Kate shifted her position so that she was close to him, close enough to feel his warmth, close enough to know that she was moving once more into danger, and reckless enough not to care. 'They're starting,' Max said softly, and she followed his glance out of the window, at the moon-bright snowscape opposite. 'Look. . .'

The first of the torches showed at the top of the ridge, below the line of fir trees. It moved along, slowly, and was joined by another, and another. Within seconds there was a long line of them, tiny points of flickering golden light. And then they began to descend, moving swiftly down the hillside in one long, straight line as their bearers *schussed* down the slope.

Almost before they reached the bottom of the hill, the next torches were appearing at the top. These came down in a different formation—criss-crossing each other's trails so that the slope became alive with shimmering lights, a pattern of yellow stars that constantly changed, broke and reformed. At the same time, Kate could see the first torches gliding aloft on the T-bar as their bearers rode up for the next descent, and kept a continual, flowing movement to the display on the open *piste*.

Now there were lights everywhere, sweeping down the long run that led along the top of the ridge and breaking away to make their own descents, on the wide bare spaces, through the narrow, tree-lined tracks, on the traverse and on the *schuss*. Several times Kate saw torches converge and was sure their bearers must crash, but each time they wheeled apart just in time. She watched, enthralled, as the hillside came to life, a teeming entity of light and colour as some of the torches began to burn with different flames; some bright blue, others a brilliant green, some acetylene white, others acid yellow. Many of the skiers were carrying two torches, so that their lights kept a parallel path; all whirled them at times, making arcs and loops and circles in the sky.

When it was finally over, Kate drew a deep breath.

She turned to Max, and her eyes were shining like the torches they had been watching on the hillside.

'What wonderful skiing!' she said, and slid quite naturally into his arms.

Max lowered his head and she felt his lips touch her hair.

'Wonderful,' he murmured huskily. 'Kate. . .'

'Don't say anything,' she begged. 'Don't talk. Just let's. . .stay like this, for a few minutes.'

He was silent. Kate felt her heart against his, kicking wildly. Her face was touching the powerful muscles of his chest; she could feel the warmth of his skin against her cheek. She turned her head slightly and felt the friction of hair against her lips. The big body quivered against her, and a flame licked heat along her limbs.

'Why just for a few minutes?' she heard him mutter, and he drew her up against him, holding her face a few inches from his so that he could look searchingly into her eyes. 'Why not for longer? A night—a week—a year. . .?'

Kate stared at him. She opened her mouth, but he was speaking again, his voice low, throbbing, urgent.

'Kate—let's stop fencing with each other. We both know we've got something special—something that can grow and develop, something that shouldn't be killed. Why do you pretend it's not there, Kate? Why don't you want to know?' His grip changed suddenly, and he caught her against him, holding her close against his bare, throbbing chest. 'Tell me you know it's there, Kate,' he insisted, his mouth hard against her cheek. 'Tell me it's the same for you.' He held her away again, and his eyes were like burning torches now, more brilliant than any they had seen on the slopes. 'Tell me. . .'

His gaze held hers. She couldn't look away, couldn't move. Couldn't deny the currrents flowing so strongly between them, the driving, urgent need of her body for his. Somewhere deep inside a voice was crying out, warning her. . .but stronger, more powerful, was the primitive instinct that drew them together so insistently, so inexorably.

'Tell me. . .' he whispered and, trembling, her heart a wild animal in her breast, her breath as fast and shallow as if she had just run a marathon, Kate nodded. It was too late now for caution, too late to assess the danger Max Sarsby might be, too late to draw back. As she had known from the beginning it would, the power of his magnetism had drawn her as surely as a flame draws a moth, and there was nothing she could do now to escape the spell he had cast on her. This moment was the culmination of countless sleepless nights, of weeks of longing. With her reason, she had tried to stave it off, tried to evade the inevitable outcome, but reason played no part now in her submission; her body was in full control.

She lifted her face for his kiss, her lips parted softly, her eyes closed. She felt his fingertips move slowly, tenderly, down the line of her cheek, her jaw, trace the shape of her mouth, touch the tip of her nose. He let them drift further, down into the hollow of her throat to encircle her slender neck, and then she felt him bend nearer and lay his mouth upon hers.

The kiss began like the touch of a butterfly, his mouth shaping itself to hers, his tongue probing in an almost tentative exploration that, nevertheless, brought fire

flaming through her body, so that she quickened in his
arms, tightening her own clasp and pressing herself
harder against that warm, quivering flesh. One hand
slid up to tangle in thick black hair which twined itself
around her fingers as sinuously as Max, laying her back
on the couch with one smooth, flowing movement, was
twining himself around her body. His lips hardened
against hers, their demands increasing, and at the same
moment she felt the hardening of his muscles against her
in a challenge that was wholly masculine. Her own
desire increased to a white heat; she moaned and twisted
in his arms, but with no wish now to escape; she wanted
only to get nearer to him, closer, to feel the rough friction
of his skin against her own smoothness, to know the
shape of him as intimately as passion could allow, to
find at last release from all the longing in an explosion
that would fill the velvet sky with iridescent colour. . .

'What was that?'

For a moment, bewildered, confused, she thought it
had happened, that the sky had indeed exploded with
the passion of their new discovery. She struggled in
Max's arms, eyes wide, gazing round at the room which
was suddenly lit with brilliant green, with red, blue,
orange and white. She shrank away from the noise that
the colour seemed to be producing—a fusillade of
crackling, of shots, of rapid cannon-fire. 'Max—what is
it?'

Max laughed gently, cradling her in his arms. 'It's
only the fireworks, Kate—had you forgotten? There's
always a fireworks display after the torchlight procession. Look. . .' he lifted her in his arms and pointed
out of the big window '. . .there's another. A rocket. And
another—and another. Oh, Kate, Kate—what a way to
find our love. What a night to discover each other!'

She turned her face into his breast again, and then lifted it for another lingering kiss, a kiss that this time followed the path his fingers had previously tracked, deep down into the hollow of her throat, and into the neck of her sweater to find the cleft between her full and tingling breasts. Fireworks! she thought dreamily, and echoed Max's words in her mind. What a night, indeed, to discover love.

She stretched herself against him, lifting her arms above her head so that her breasts stood out invitingly, and Max swiftly lifted her sweater and peeled it away from her slender body. She saw his eyes fall on the swelling globes in their fragile encasing of black lace, and then, with a muffled groan, he dropped his face against them, covering them with a series of kisses— tiny, pecking kisses, searching kisses and, finally, kisses that took the whole of her erect nipple into his mouth in tender, passionate supplication.

Kate twisted frantically from side to side. Around her, the sky was exploding with colour and sound, and it seemed to her that her whole body was doing the same— a violent disruption of her entire being, a savage splintering of sensation that she could no longer hope to control. Max's kisses, his increasingly intimate caresses that were now taking in her whole body, sweeping from the blonde hair that tangled around his wrist, down the whole shivering length of her to the tips of her quivering toes, were driving her to the brink of an abyss—an abyss she had only dreamed of, an abyss beyond which there was a complete new world of erotic delight and consummate ecstasy.

'Max. . .' she whimpered against his mouth when he lifted his head from her breasts at last. 'Max. . .I can't bear it. . .please, Max, have mercy. . .' But even as she uttered the words, she knew that it wasn't mercy she wanted, but only a greater and more urgent force, a force even more impossible to resist, that would bring her to the brink of that abyss and hurl her over it with one final, devastating thrust, so that, falling, she would cling to Max as her lifeline and know that this was forever—a peak which they could only reach together, a descent that would always bring them peace.

There was a final, shattering crash from outside. Max slid his hand down her body once more and then, with a kiss whose tenderness quietened her raging body, lifted himself gently away from her.

Kate lay quite still on the white cushions, watching him. The aurora of colour faded from the sky. The room was filled once again with shadows.

'Max?' she whispered at last, and reached up a tentative hand to touch him.

He turned and looked down at her, but his face was hidden by the darkness and she could not read his expression.

'Max? What are you thinking?' Her voice was soft, languorous; the pinnacle of passion had levelled out, become a wide, blissful plateau, a resting-place before the climax of a love she had battled against and could fight no longer. She was ready, gloriously ready now, to submit. She let her finger trail gently down his cheek, his neck, into the deep V of his ski-suit.

He moved restlessly and caught her hand, holding it close against him. To her surprise, she saw that his eyes were burning now with a different passion. A tiny spring of fear uncoiled itself deep in her stomach and she moved suddenly, raising herself against him. 'Max. . .?'

The dark blue eyes were blazing into hers, and his face was alight. But he was staring at her as if he saw something else—a vision of which she was only a part.

'Kate. . .do you know what you've done for me? Have you any idea?' He gripped her, pulling her close against his hard, warm body. 'Kate, you've given me the world! With you beside me, I can do anything, anything. I can win that trophy, Kate!' He was almost incandescent, but Kate, staring into the eyes that were burning so close to hers, felt suddenly chilled. 'With you at my side, nothing—nobody—can beat me!'

Kate felt her body grow cold. Only moments before, she could have sworn that his attention had been concentrated entirely on her. In his arms, believing that he must love her as she loved him, even though he had not yet spoken the words, she had been ready to give herself entirely. And now—now he had forgotten her, forgotten the desire that had brought them together, swept it all aside in his obsession with the championship he was so determined to win. He sees me as nothing more than an aid to victory, she thought in disbelief, and wrenched herself from his arms.

He stared at her blankly. 'Kate. . .'

'Let me alone!' she panted, retreating to the other end of the sofa. 'Don't touch me!' She could see bewilderment dawning in his eyes, but panic was sweeping through her body now and she was beyond reason. He'll never understand, she thought despairingly. Even if I were to tell him about David. . .he'd never understand. Different though they might appear—the one so fair, the other so dark, the one a musical genius, the other an athlete— their basic make-up was the same. They were both possessed of this terrible need, this urge to be the best,

at whatever cost. A parent's death, a near-fatal accident—nothing could stop men like these two. And it was
her misfortune to be attracted to such men—men who
could only spell doom.

'Kate. . .' he said again, and his arms reached out
once more.

'No! No!' Frantically, she scrabbled for her sweater.
'I'm not here to help you win trophies,' she gasped, and
knew that her words sounded lame.

'Kate—what in hell's name is the matter? What are
you talking about? You know about me—you know why
I'm here. You must understand the need I have to win.
It means spending the summer on the glaciers, training
hard. It means gym work, every day. It means giving
my whole heart and soul and body to getting fit for the
next winter's championships.' His hands tightened on
hers, so that she almost cried out, but she was watching
him now with fear in her eyes, and could not utter a
sound. 'I've got to win that championship next season,'
he muttered, almost as if to himself. 'Until I've done
that, nothing else matters. Nothing else can be *allowed* to
matter. Can't you understand that, Kate? Can't you
accept it?'

Kate stared at him. His face had changed, twisting
into a tortured mask that struck terror into her heart.
How could any man be sane, when driven by such a
consuming ambition? How could any mere trophy
matter so much? Fear crept into her heart, grew, became
panic. With a sudden movement, she wrenched her
hands from his grasp and kicked herself free of him and
off the couch. Keeping her eyes on him, she made a grab
for her sweater and pulled it with shaking hands over
her head.

'No, Max,' she said, and her voice was shaking with the stress of all that had happened since she had first entered this room. 'No, I can't understand it—I can't accept it. I've never understood the competitive urge and, when it reaches the extent it has in you, I think it's more than an obsession—it's a kind of madness.' She found her jacket and thrust her arms into the sleeves. 'I'm sorry, Max—I daren't love a man who believes the world begins and ends with skiing—or any other sport. There must be something else you can do with your life—something really worthwhile.' She held out her hand. 'Give me the key, Max. I'd like to leave now. And—please—don't ever come near me again. I've always known you were bad news. This evening has proved it.'

Without looking at her, Max felt in the pocket of his ski-suit and handed her the key. She walked across the room and unlocked the door.

As it swung open, letting a shaft of light flood into the darkened room, she glanced back. Max was standing at the window, his back stiff. For a brief second, she was on the point of running back to him, telling him she would follow wherever he led.

And then she thought again of David. And walked out.

CHAPTER NINE

KATE slept very little that night, and when she did doze her mind was still filled with Max. He appeared in a series of confused dreams, confronting her sometimes with anger and sometimes with love. From the one, she woke with a face wet with tears; from the other, she came slowly back to consciousness, convinced that she could feel his arms around her, the shape of his body pressed close against her own, the cool firmness of his lips on her cheek.

She was almost thankful when her alarm went off at five and she had to get up. Today was her busiest day— the day of 'transfers', when most of her guests went back to England and a new batch arrived. It was the day when almost anything could go wrong, and frequently did—from a simple mistake made earlier in the week, which had meant there were not enough coaches to carry everyone, to a decision made hundreds of miles away which resulted in the entire plane-load being severely delayed. This was what every rep dreaded most—and, as Kate might have known, this was what had happened today.

'There's a strike of some kind at Manchester Airport,' she was told when she telephoned Salzburg just before leaving to collect her first departures of the day—half a dozen people who had come all the way by road and would be taken by taxi to join the main coach at St Johann. 'Passengers travelling from there are being transported to Leeds and Bradford. We don't know yet what the final delay time will be.'

Kate groaned. After last night's culmination of all the emotional turmoil of the past weeks, this was all she needed. But there was nothing she could do about it. Her guests would have to leave at the arranged time, even though she knew there would be a long wait for some of them at the airport. Not all of them were flying to Manchester, and other people who needed to get to Salzburg for their flights would be joining their coaches *en route* too. She would just have to explain as best she could and, if the delay looked like being a long one, arrange for a meal of some kind to be served to them while they waited.

She trudged through the dark, icy streets to meet her first departures, who were waiting in disconsolate little groups in hotel foyers, their luggage piled around their feet. Kate greeted them with the smile that even this morning she had to dredge up from somewhere, and they returned her greeting rather wanly. Most of them had enjoyed themselves to the full during yesterday's celebrations, and were now paying the price. Too much *schnapps* at the fondue party last night, she thought, glancing at one or two particularly white faces, and spared them a moment's sympathy for the rigours of the journey ahead.

All they needed was for the taxi to fail to turn up, and the day would be off to a *really* good start!

Fortunately, there was no such hitch. Kate saw her guests off, waving them goodbye with a cheerfulness she did not feel, and smiling until she felt her face would crack as they all promised to see her again the next year. The taxi disappeared into the darkness and she turned to trudge back to the Brunners' house, where she would have an early breakfast and then return for the main group, who would be going by coach.

This was the moment she had been dreading. The thought of facing Max over breakfast this morning was one that had haunted her throughout the night. She was almost tempted to forgo the meal entirely, but knew that this would be foolish in the extreme—Sunday was the one day when she needed to leave the house with a good meal inside her, for there was no knowing when or what her next one might be! She took a deep breath and went into the Brunners' warm and colourful kitchen.

Frau Brunner was there alone, setting warm rolls in a basket. She put them on the table as Kate entered, and smiled.

'So. It's a busy day for you. I have some good cheese here, and some cornflakes—eat plenty, now.'

'Thank you, Frau Brunner.' Kate filled a bowl with cornflakes, wondering just how she was going to eat them. 'Max is still sleeping?'

'But no!' Frau Brunner looked concerned. Max was usually first in the kitchen at breakfast-time, eager to be out on the slopes as soon as the lifts opened. Kate, who had usually been late to bed because of one of her evening activities—the bob-sleighing she arranged, the bowling, or the folklore evening—normally breakfasted later, so had often been able to avoid him. 'He is not in his room—he did not come home last night.'

'Didn't come home?' Kate looked at her in surprise and then, before she could stop herself, thought of Helga. Had he invited the German girl up to that sumptuous room, after the encounter there with Kate? The thought sickened her—and yet, what else could have happened?

She had left Max in a state of acute frustration—perhaps humiliation, perhaps anger, she didn't know. But what more likely than that he should have reacted as extremely as she had herself in her rejection of him, and gone straight to the arms of a woman who *would* support his ambitions—the woman who had already made clear her determination to possess him?

'I suppose he met some friends and stayed with them,' she said lamely. 'He did say he had a friend coming to stay in the village.'

'Yes, I dare say that's it,' Frau Brunner said. 'And it is common after the day of the village race and the parties at night—there are often young men who do not come home.' She smiled at Kate and Kate returned the smile weakly. 'And Max is a grown man, with much experience—he does not have to account to me for his actions.'

She poured Kate's coffee and they sat companionably together, eating their breakfast. It was quiet in the warm kitchen; the tiled stove gave off a steady heat, and the coloured table-cloth with its array of rolls, cheeses and fruit preserves looked welcoming and peaceful. Did Frau Brunner ever suffer the kind of emotional upheaval I've been going through ever since I arrived here? Kate wondered. Looking at the plump figure with its serene, rosy face, it seemed impossible to imagine. And yet few people went through life without any trouble at all, without any heartache or tragedy. It was how you coped with it that was important.

Well, and couldn't she cope with this? After all, she'd walked into trouble with her eyes wide open. She'd *known* Max Sarsby could never be any good to her. And she'd known that there was an attraction there that would, given a chance, prove too powerful for her to handle. So she'd been foolish enough to give it that chance—tempted almost beyond her strength—and, just as she'd foreseen, it had brought trouble.

But at least she'd had the sense last night to get out of it before her submission had been complete. And she wouldn't let anything like it happen again, that was for sure. From now on, Max would be kept severely at a distance. And it didn't have to be for long—in a few weeks now the season would be over, and they would both leave the village. And she, for one, would never come back; she was never going to take the risk of meeting Max Sarsby again.

It was late when Kate, exhausted almost to the point of sleepwalking, arrived back at St Joachim. The day had been one that reps have nightmares about—a day that it had seemed would never end.

By the time the coach had arrived at Salzburg, it had been buzzing with rumours about the strike at Manchester. Some people had heard brief mentions of it on their radios, but no one had the full story or knew how it was likely to affect them, and all expected Kate to answer their questions.

'I'm sorry,' she kept saying, 'I don't know any more than you do. I won't be able to tell you any more until we get to the airport. If all of you who are going to Manchester will just stay in the coach for a few minutes while I go to investigate. . .' They wouldn't, she knew that. There were always a few who would insist on making their own investigations, disappearing the moment her back was turned, and others who would need to make immediate visits to the toilets after their journey, even though there had been a brief stop on the way. By the time she had made her enquiries and set up any alternative arrangements that needed to be made, she would be lucky to have half her passengers left. But, short of locking the door on them, there was little she could do about it.

'I'll be as quick as I can,' she said, going down the steps as soon as the coach door swung open. But even as she went through the big glass doors of the airport, she could see that three men were already getting out. Bother you! she thought, recognising them as guests who had been extra querulous during the whole of the previous week, complaining about anything and everything. And then, in a moment of rebellion—oh, well, get lost if that's what you want! Why should I care if you miss your flight?

But she did care, all the same. Kate took her responsibilities very seriously. All the guests had paid hard-earned money for their skiing holidays; all deserved the best treatment she could obtain for them. And, tired and unhappy as she might be, her own personal problems had no place here, where her first concern must be for the people who looked to her to solve theirs.

The strike, they told her when she asked, was by staff at Manchester airport. While they were refusing to work, no aircraft could either take off or land. Passengers in England were being asked to check in at the airport as usual; then, when they should have been taking off, they were being transported by coach to the airport between Leeds and Bradford, where their own flights had to be slotted in between the flights already scheduled there. This meant that they were at least three hours late in taking off, and it could be more.

Since the same plane was used to bring Manchester-bound passengers back from Salzburg, the guests waiting to go home faced a similar delay—and, at the end of their flight, a long coach journey back to Manchester, where many of them had left their cars or were being met.

It was a depressing end to anyone's holiday, Kate knew. And it was up to her to make it as little trouble as possible for them.

In cases like this, she was able to arrange a snack or meal in the airport, at the company's expense. She went back to the coach to report.

As she had expected, several of the Manchester-bound passengers had disappeared. But they could be located inside the airport building; after all, she thought grimly, there were at least three hours available in which to contact them. She gave the rest of the waiting guests her news and, predictably, they groaned loudly.

'But you can all have a snack while you're waiting,' she announced. 'I've got vouchers here. . .You're entitled to a drink, whatever you like, and something to eat—it *is* only a snack, not a four-course meal, but you'll be served a meal on the plane, of course. . . If the delay is any longer than three hours, I may be able to arrange something more, but I don't think it should be. . . Has anyone any questions?'

'Can't we go into Salzburg for an hour or two?' someone asked, and Kate suppressed a groan. Let them loose in the city? She would never get them all back together again! She shook her head firmly.

'It's too far away. And there's no transport, only taxis. It wouldn't be worth it for the short time you'd get there.

No, I'm afraid you'll have to stay in the airport. I'm sorry—it's a bore, I know. But it can't be helped.'

'Perhaps we could use the coach?' someone else suggested, but Kate pretended she hadn't heard that, and the suggestion wasn't repeated. She glanced at her list.

'If any of you see the Thompsons, or Mr Medway, I'd be grateful if you could let them know what's happening. Tell them I've got their vouchers here. And we need to have their luggage out of the coach, too—Hans can't stay parked here much longer.'

'Do you mean we have to tote our luggage around in there for three hours?' one of the women asked in dismay. 'We've got our own skis, too—we can't carry them about.'

'No, you can all go through the check-in at once. The airport isn't busy—don't forget, there's no flight in from Manchester yet, so until that arrives they're pretty slack.' Kate folded her papers away with a determined air. 'I'm sorry, there really isn't any more that I can do, and the delay isn't so very long—think of those people in Spain last summer, held up for twenty-four hours or more! Now, if you'd like to come and collect your vouchers, Hans will open up the luggage compartment. . .' She breathed a sigh of relief as they shrugged and then began to get out of their seats. She couldn't blame them for being irritated—nobody liked being held up, and no doubt in many cases they were concerned, too, about people meeting them at home. But none of them had grown angry, or blamed her, as sometimes happened. Some guests seemed to take a delight in laying everything at the rep's door, and using her as a scapegoat when things went wrong.

She watched the passengers collect their luggage and

disappear into the airport building, some of them clearly disconsolate, others taking a philosophical view of it all. But she didn't have any more time to spend on them just yet; there were passengers for other airports to be checked, to make sure they were all in the right place to board their own planes. And even then, there was only a brief lull in which to relax a little with a cup of coffee and the other reps.

'What a bind this is!' Julie observed as they sat down to compare notes on the past week. 'And the next thing is breaking the news to people from Gatwick and Heathrow and Birmingham that they've got to wait three hours for the Manchester flight to come in before we can leave Salzburg! Still, at least they'll know about the strike—it started two or three days ago, I believe.'

'They won't have connected it with themselves, though,' Kate said gloomily. 'People never do. They won't realise that a strike at Manchester could affect their arrival in Salzburg. Or, at least, their journey to their ski resort. And they're bound to blame us.'

'Well, that's what we're for!' Julie grinned. 'Whipping-boys. Are you all right, Kate? You seem a bit down.'

'I'm OK. Just tired.'

Julie gave her a shrewd glance. 'Hmm. And how's the great Sarsby?'

Kate felt her colour deepen. 'Fine, so far as I know. Why?'

'Because I've got more than a suspicion that he's been getting to you in some way. It's the way you react whenever his name's mentioned, Kate. And you've been staying in the same house with him for months now.

You ought to have got used to him—but you never have.'

'Got used to him?' Kate laughed shortly. 'I don't think anyone could ever get used to Max Sarsby.'

'Correction. Most people can get used to anyone.' Julie's brown eyes rested thoughtfully on Kate's face. 'You either hate the man, Kate—or you love him. Blowed if I can make out which.'

'Well, here's the short answer. I hate him—no, I don't even do that. I'm completely indifferent to the man. Is that good enough?' She stirred her coffee with short, fierce strokes.

Julie watched her for a moment, then shook her head. 'No, Kate, it's not good enough. And I'll tell you something else—you'll crack up if you don't talk to someone about it.' She reached across the table and touched Kate's hand. 'Why don't you let go, Kate? Stop bottling it all up. Tell me what's bugging you. I'm not a chatterer, you know. I won't spread it around—whatever it is. But I'm sure it will help you to talk.'

Kate hesitated. She wanted badly, she realised, to do just that—pour out everything that was in her heart, all the grief and pain and disillusionment that she'd had to keep to herself. I'll always need someone, she thought with a cold, bleak loneliness. And the thought of Max was sharp in her mind; sharp and agonisingly painful.

'Talk to me,' Julie said softly. 'I promise I'll never mention it again, if you don't want me to. But the way you look this morning, Kate—I think you need it.'

They had half an hour to wait for the next plane, when the airport would suddenly burst into activity, people pouring through Customs, bright-eyed and eager, looking for their coaches, expecting to be on the slopes in a matter of hours. . .There wouldn't be another chance; she wouldn't see Julie again, to talk to, until next Sunday. And Kate knew, quite suddenly, that she wouldn't be able to wait that long.

Was half an hour long enough to tell a life history? She shook her head. But the main parts—the parts that mattered. . . At least she could try.

She began to talk, and Julie listened. At first, the words came with difficulty; Kate had never been accustomed to sharing her troubles. But as she spoke, she found it easier to express her feelings, easier to tell Julie everything that had happened; her relationship with David, her dismay when she had discovered the extent of his ambition, her feelings about Max, the strength of the attraction between them, her fear of his ambition, so like David's, and what it might do to him—and to her.

'But surely that's different?' Julie said at last. 'David Julian—well, I've heard of him, of course—I've even got some of his records, the jazz ones. But he's not like Max Sarsby. His ambition's for a lifetime. He'll never stop playing the violin. And he *is* a genius. You have to admit that.'

'Oh, I admit it,' Kate said colourlessly. 'I spent a whole summer with him. There's no denying he's a genius.'

'Well, then, I think you have to admit that a genius is different from other people. And—I know he seemed callous over his reaction to his father's death—but, well, I've always felt that people with that kind of talent—they have to be *allowed* to be different. You can't expect normal behaviour from them because they have some kind of—well, if you like, some kind of higher responsibility. David Julian's responsibility is to music. He knew that. He knew that his mother knew it, too—didn't you say he told you that his parents sacrificed a lot to help him get on? I'm sure he grieved for his father, I'm sure he would have *liked* to be with his mother. But his responsibility to his music—his genius—came before that. Before anything.'

'Oh, he said that himself,' Kate said, the bitterness of that day still sounding in her voice. 'He told me it would always come first. He told me he needed an uncluttered life—we'd never have children, never have a real home. He was quite clear about that.'

'Then you can't say he wasn't honest with you,' Julie said quietly.

Kate was silent. Was Julie saying that David had been right—that she'd been wrong? That, by leaving him, she had let him down? That if you loved a genius you must automatically give up all possibility of a normal life and live only to serve whatever god it was he served?

'Look,' Julie said, a note of firmness in her voice, 'I'm not telling you you shouldn't have done what you did. If David's view of life didn't chime in with yours, then of course you had to break away. Trying to stay together would have been disaster for both of you. But you were really only doing the same as he was, weren't you? You were expecting him to live the kind of life *you* wanted. You wanted him to fit in with you. And when you saw he couldn't——'

'Oh, hell,' Kate said. 'You make me sound as selfish and as callous as he——'

'No, I *don't*. Because you're not selfish or callous, Kate—nobody could say that. But—I don't think he was, either. Not really. And I think if you can only bring yourself to see that, you could save yourself a lot more trouble in the future. And a lot of bitterness.'

Kate was silent for a while. She couldn't take in Julie's words all at once. She needed time to digest them, to turn them over in her mind. 'And what about Max?' she asked at last, her voice tight. 'Should I give myself up to *his* genius as well? Spend my life helping his ambitions?'

'But, as I said, they're completely different.' Julie frowned a little. 'Max is a skier—a fantastic one, yes, even a genius, if you can be a genius at skiing. But it's not something he's going to do all his life, is it? Champion skiers are young men, Kate. They retire at around thirty. Max is past thirty now—he hasn't got much longer. Next season will probably be his last in competitive skiing. After that, he'll have to do something different. Do you know what that's going to be?'

Kate shrugged. 'He hasn't talked about it much. All he seems to think about is his skiing.'

'Well, I suppose that's natural, when next year is the last chance he'll get to win that trophy. Look——' Julie leaned forward '——I know what I told you when we first talked about Max Sarsby. I told you what I'd heard— that he was determined to win, and that he wouldn't care who he kicked off the ladder on the way up. But from what I've seen and heard of him since, I don't think that's true. He doesn't strike me that way. He's a serious man, Max Sarsby, and I don't think he *is* going for this trophy for personal glory. I think he's got some other reason.' She paused. 'Why don't you try to find out what it is?'

Kate moved restlessly. Julie was going too fast for her now. She hadn't heard Max last night, talking about his ambition; she hadn't seen the glow in his burning eyes, felt the tension and excitement in his grasp.

'I don't know,' she said slowly. 'You may be right—but what other reason could he have? Why should anyone want to win a ski championship, if not for their own satisfaction?'

'I don't know,' Julie said. 'But I think you ought to ask. Max Sarsby didn't fight his way back from those terrible injuries without some very good reason. I just wonder why he hasn't told you what it is.'

Because I never gave him a chance, Kate realised with a pang of guilt. Because as soon as he began to talk, I panicked. I remembered David and the pain I felt after our break-up, and I wasn't prepared to risk that kind of hurt again. So I stopped Max talking, and I got out, fast.

And said a lot of things that, even now, I'm beginning to regret.

Kate got through the rest of that long and trying day with difficulty. Nothing, it seemed to her, was more important than getting back to Max, to ask him the question that now filled her mind—why, just *why* was it so important to him to win that championship? What had made it the most important thing in his life?

The answer might not be to her liking. It might still turn out that Max Sarsby was really only out for his own glory. But the more Kate thought about it, the more sure she became that there was more to it than that. Julie was right. Max was a different kind of person from David Julian. David had been as finely tuned as the violin he played so magnificently, his whole being honed towards one end—that of being the finest violinist the

world had ever known. Nothing else had mattered to
him but that; when the chips were down he would
always—as when his father had died—put his music
first.

But Max didn't have that frightening single-mindedness. He trained with determination, pushed himself to
the limits, but—there was the difference, Kate realised.
Max knew what he could achieve, and he pushed himself
to achieve it. David did not have to push—it was almost
as if he *was* pushed. By some force that was beyond his
control, a force he went along with because there was no
other choice.

Max had already shown, by the way he had joined in
the village race, by the liking the villagers had for him,
that he was a normal man, enjoying normal pleasures.
David had lived on his own plane, and the woman who
chose to share his life would have to live on that plane,
too.

Kate hadn't been able to accept that—but it didn't
mean David's way was wrong. Simply that it was wrong
for her.

And Max's way? What had he offered her? After the
next year was over, when he had done what he set out
to do and won his championship, what then? Did he see
her as someone permanent in his life?

She didn't know. Because she hadn't given him a
chance to tell her.

The first flight of the day arrived, from Gatwick. Kate
and Julie watched from the viewing window as the plane
taxied along the runway and came to a stop. They saw
the steps being wheeled into position and the doors open.
There were already photographers at the bottom of the
steps, ready to snap each passenger coming down. The

passengers looked happy and excited; they weren't aware of being photographed, and the prints, displayed on their return to the airport in a week's or a fortnight's time, would come as a surprise.

'They won't look so pleased when we tell them they have to wait two hours for the Manchester flight to arrive,' Julie remarked. 'Well, it's a good chance to practise our skills in public relations! Here we go, Kate. Good luck—and good luck during the week, too.'

'Thanks. And thanks for letting me talk.' Kate smiled ruefully. 'I don't know if you were really prepared for all that—but it did help. And you've given me something to think about, too.'

'Think nothing of it.' The other girl gave an airy wave of her hand and then turned away. 'Better make tracks—they'll be through Customs any minute now. See you, Kate!'

She disappeared towards the Arrivals hall, and Kate followed more slowly, her mind still busy with new and disturbing thoughts. Then she shook herself. There was work to be done—a hundred or more skiers arriving, to be sorted into different coaches, taken to a variety of destinations, their queries and problems sorted out, their anxieties and irritations soothed. It would be a long time before she was able to think clearly again about her own affairs.

And she was almost too tired to walk when she finally trudged along the frozen road to Frau Brunner's house. She wanted nothing more than to fall into bed and sleep—preferably for several days. But first, she wanted badly to see Max.

It wasn't a good idea to start talking again now, she knew that. Not when she was as exhausted as this; not after such a day as she had just had. But talking wasn't what she wanted. She just wanted to see him. To look into those deep blue eyes, to feel those strong arms around her, the broad, hard body pressed close against hers. She just wanted to whisper that she was sorry; that they'd talk again, later, and that this time she would try to understand.

But even as she entered the house, stepping wearily into the dimly lit hall, she knew that there was to be no Max that night. And when she heard a movement from the kitchen and looked up, her heart leaping with sudden hope, to see Frau Brunner coming out with a face that looked almost as tired and despondent as her own, she knew that she had left it too late.

'Frau Brunner?' she asked, her voice little more than a thread. 'What is it? What's wrong? Has anything happened?'

'It's Max,' the Austrian woman said, and her face was as piteous as that of a mother who has watched her son march out of her life. 'He left this morning. He came home at about ten o'clock, and he packed all his things and left. He says he won't be coming back to St Joachim—ever.' She shook her head. 'We were fond of him here, Kate. All the people liked him. Something must have happened at the party last night, but nobody knows what it was—nobody even saw him. And now he has gone.'

'Gone!' Kate felt her body grow cold. She knew what had happened; she knew why Max Sarsby had left the village he had loved. And she knew that it wasn't just St Joachim he had left for ever—it was her.

'And there's something else,' the older woman went on. 'He didn't go alone. The German girl—Helga—

went with him.' She lifted her eyes to Kate's. 'That girl is no good to him, Kate. She thinks only of what he will be—a champion. She does not love him for what he is.'

'What he is?' Kate repeated dully. 'And what's that, Frau Brunner?'

'Why, he is a man,' Frau Brunner said simply. 'A very fine man, but still—just a man. A man who can ski.'

A man who could ski. Wasn't that, more or less, what Julie had implied? That Max was a normal man who could, when he tried, achieve just that little bit more than other men could? A man who could ski—but didn't look on it as his reason for living.

What would Helga do when Max had won his championship and returned to normal life? Would she—in spite of Frau Brunner's doubts—love him for whatever he was then?

A sudden rage rose up in Kate—rage that she had wasted so much time in bitterness, that she had never looked deeply enough into her own motives to understand why she had really left David, why she was afraid of Max. There had been nothing to fear at all—she saw that now. Only the possibility that she might lose him—as now, through her own idiotic foolishness, she had.

She turned away and went slowly, dispiritedly, up to her room. Max had gone, believing that she did not love him. He could not be blamed for taking with him the woman who did seem to share his aspirations. And it would be no use for Kate to follow him now; Max Sarsby had his own pride and his own limits, and the fact that he had left said clearly enough what reception he would give her if she did.

No. She had lost Max for good. And only a few hours after she had found him.

CHAPTER TEN

THE season came to an end abruptly only a few weeks later, when the sun began to shine with increased heat, the temperatures rose and the snow melted. The villagers of St Joachim greeted the rapidly filling river and the emerging green grass with both resignation and cheerfulness; resignation because, even after several months of non-stop activity, they were still sorry to be putting away their boots and skis for the summer; cheerfulness because it would, after all, be rather pleasant to bask in warmth for a while, to swim in the lake that had been frozen all winter, and to welcome visitors who came for a lazier holiday, and were happy to walk on the tracks that had been used as *pistes* and to take leisurely excursions to villages that had been almost impossible to reach during the winter.

Kate needed little time to wind up her own affairs. Stanton's ran holidays to St Joachim in the summer as well as the winter, but she had already requested a holiday of her own, and then a change of resort. In fact, as she told Frank Dawson when she returned to London, she would really rather not go back there at all.

'It did me good, just as you said it would,' she said, sitting in his airy modern office. 'I even got back on my skis—and I laid a lot of ghosts.' She bit her lip, thinking that some of those ghosts—the ones concerning David Julian especially—had been laid too late. 'But I'd really

rather go somewhere different next year. Somewhere a
bit bigger, perhaps. Livelier.'

'Bigger? Livelier? You surprise me, Kate—I didn't
think that was your scene. Still, I'll see what I can
do. . .' He stared at the big map on his wall and screwed
up his mouth. 'Anyway, no rush to decide that. You'll
be having your own holiday first. Any ideas about that?'

Kate laughed. 'You wouldn't be trying to sell me
something? No, I'm staying here for this one, Frank.
Don't forget, I spent most of my childhood abroad—and
being at boarding school doesn't exactly have the same
effect as living here full time. The only part of England
I really know is a tiny corner of Worcestershire. Sometimes I feel like a foreigner in my own country. . . I'm
going to spend some time in Wales with my parents first.
And then I'm going to Scotland for some walking.' And
to get Max Sarsby out of my system, she added silently.
There had been too many sleepless nights lately; she'd
lost weight, and was conscious of dark circles under her
eyes. Living in St Joachim after Max had left had been
a particularly exquisite form of torture, she'd decided,
and there had been no chance of forgetting him while
she still expected to meet him round the next corner, out
on the slopes or in Frau Brunner's house. Perhaps in a
different place, with a different kind of scenery, she
might begin to find peace.

'Right. Hope you have a good time. And then. . .'
Frank drew a sheet of paper from under the pile on his
desk '. . .maybe you'd like to tackle this. Greece—nice
and warm and sunny. Only for the last half of the
season—present rep's getting married. Suit you?'

'Greece!' Kate's face lit up. 'Frank, that'd be marvellous. I've only done the one season there—what was it

now, three or four years ago?—but I loved every minute of it. Yes, I'd like to do that.'

'OK, we'll consider it settled.' Frank's heavy face settled into a smile as he looked at her. 'I'm proud of you, Kate,' he said. 'You've done well. Pulled yourself through a very nasty patch. I think things will go well for you from now on.'

Kate stared at him for a moment. Did he really not see the truth—that she was eating her heart out for a man whom she had, in a moment of blind panic, turned away? Did he really not recognise the pain she was suffering even at this moment—the pain she carried with her wherever she went?

But why should he? She tried hard enough to keep it hidden. She could scarcely blame Frank Dawson, who was kindly but not particularly perceptive, for not seeing what she took such trouble to conceal.

'I'll be going now, Frank,' she said at last. 'Thanks for everything. I'll see you again before I go to Greece, and meanwhile this address will find me.' She gave him her father's address. 'And—thanks again for insisting I went to Austria last winter. You were right—it was just what I needed.'

Even if it had brought more than either she or Frank had bargained for, that was true. Because if she hadn't gone to St Joachim—if she hadn't met Max Sarsby— she would never have had his example to inspire her to ski again. And she might have carried the fear and the sorrow of her cousins' deaths with her for the rest of her days.

It had crippled her, just as her feelings about David Julian had crippled her. Just as—if she were not care- ful—her unhappiness over Max might cripple her now.

It mustn't happen, Kate decided as she left Frank's office and walked out into the bustle and noise of Piccadilly. If she had learned anything from her winter in Austria, it had been to go forward in life. Not to be crushed by it.

Max had not allowed his misfortunes to crush him. If she loved him at all—and she did, more now than ever, even though she knew it could never be fulfilled—she must continue to follow his example. And that meant not giving in. Never giving in.

A holiday in Wales. A walking tour in Scotland. And then the rest of the summer in Greece.

Surely that ought to be enough to help anyone get back in control of their life?

Kate returned to Frank Dawson's office at the beginning of October. She was still thinner than before, her slender waist looking almost brittle, but she was brown and glowing, and her hair had bleached almost silver in the Greek sun. Her green eyes still had a touch of the sea in them, and more than one head turned as she walked down the street and into the office of Stanton Holidays.

'Well, Frank? Where are you sending me?' She smiled at him, knowing that wherever it was, she could cope. She'd had a summer without Max and she'd taught herself to live without him. It hadn't been easy—there had been many, many nights when she had slept on a pillow wet with tears—but she'd survived and intended to go on surviving. So long as she didn't have to go back to St Joachim again. . .

Frank gave her an admiring grin. 'Kate, you look lovelier than ever. I don't know why you stick with this job—you could be a model, a film star, anything!'

Kate smiled back. 'You think so? Being a model means having to keep still for more than five minutes at a time, and I could never do that! And being a film star means being able to act—and I can't do that, either. No, all I'm fit for is being a rep, I'm afraid. Having a few languages, which is nothing clever when you grew up the way I did, and an ability to organise, which most women have anyway, as part of their natural equipment, what else *could* I have been?'

Frank laughed. 'Have it your own way, although I think you're being excessively modest. . . Anyway, here's your new assignment. Sorry it's a bit last-minute—as you know, we'd intended you to go to Kitzbühel, but one of the other reps has been taken ill, and the only other one I could send isn't really up to this job. So we're sending her to Kitz, and you to the other one.' His eyes crinkled. 'I hope you'll like it, Kate. You did ask for something bigger.'

'Something bigger?' Kate stretched out her hand. 'But Kitzbühel's bigger than St. . .' Her eyes dropped to the sheet of paper he had just handed her, and she gasped. 'Frank! You can't mean it! Crans Montana! But that's where the—where they're holding the——'

'World skiing championships. I know.' His face was solemn, his eyes twinkling. 'It's going to be a busy winter there, Kate, and hard work for reps. That's why we only send our best.' He grinned again. 'You did ask for something lively!'

Lively! Crans Montana would certainly be that, she thought, and sat down slowly. Did Frank have any idea what he was doing to her? Did he have any notion at all of what he was sending her to?

Max Sarsby was almost certain to be at Crans
Montana for those championships. If he'd continueed
with his training during the summer with glacier-skiing,
as he'd told her he intended, he should be as ready as
anyone to take part—ready to win. At the end of
January, he would be there with all the others, the
attention of the skiing world focused on him as he
swooped and twisted his way down the mountain course
towards the victory he was certain was his. And she
would be there, watching.

It didn't mean they were bound to meet, she reasoned
with herself, fighting the panic that rose in her at the
thought of another encounter with Max. Holiday reps
and championship competitors lived in different worlds.
Crans Montana was no tiny village—indeed, it was two
villages, and the biggest skiing area Switzerland could
offer. And while the championships were on, its ordinary
population of locals and visitors would be expanded by
over thirty thousand spectators, competitors, officials
and Press representatives. It was hardly likely that she
would come face to face with Max in that throng!

All the same. . . Emotions churned uncomfortably
within her. Did she dare to go to Crans Montana, on
even the slightest chance that they might, somehow,
meet?

Or—to put the question another way—did she dare
not to go. . .?

Of course, she went. There had never been any doubt
about it, Kate realised as she walked into the apartment
she was to share with several other reps and dropped
her luggage on the floor.

She crossed to the window and stared out. The streets

were crowded with people, for Crans Montana was a popular resort even when not hosting the World Championships. Later, it would become even busier; later, she might look out just as she was doing now and see Max Sarsby walking down the street towards her.

Max. Kate sat in one of the chairs and stared unseeingly around the room. Since discovering she was coming here, she had made a few enquiries, and found that Max had indeed spent the summer glacier-skiing and training for the winter season. Already his entry for the championship races was known, and he was being discussed as a possible hope for Britain. Those discussing him took sharply different views—some saw him as the biggest hope Britain had ever had in the races that were almost invariably won by Continentals. Others dismissed his chances: it was too long since he had last raced, he'd been too badly injured ever to recover his old form, he was too old, anyway, and would have lost the flexibility and muscular power he had shown in his early days.

'Sarsby?' someone had said with a laugh. 'A lost cause! He'd be better off back in that hospital he talks so much about.'

What hospital? Kate wanted to ask, but she didn't want anyone to know that she had a special interest in Max. It must be the hospital which had treated him after his accident. But—talked so much about it? He'd hardly mentioned it to her. . .

But then, she'd never given him all that much chance to mention anything, had she? And maybe that had been the problem. Maybe they hadn't talked enough—had spent too much time either arguing or. . .or almost making love.

Almost. The story of my life, she thought bitterly. The

almost girl. If only they *had* made love. If only she'd had
the courage to let herself go, to trust him with her body,
with herself—would things be any different now? Would
they then have found time to talk, so that he could have
told her what was in his mind, so that she could have
welcomed him into her heart?

Sighing, she got to her feet and carried her luggage
into the room assigned to her. And wondered where
Helga was figuring in all this.

Was she still with Max? Providing him with the
support he'd said he needed—the support he'd asked
Kate for?

Was she as likely to bump into Helga as Max?

Crans Montana was, as Frank had said, both busy and
lively. As well as the normal skiers, who began to arrive
just before Christmas, the slopes were alive with people
who were concerned with the coming championship
races. The racing *pistes* had to be decided upon, marked
out, and carefully prepared, the early fall of snow
forming a base which would be tended with all the care
of a groundsman preparing his grass for tennis or cricket,
the snow rolled and pressed until it was rock-hard, as
smooth as glass, without a bump or rut to be seen on the
shining surface, which now needed only light falls of
snow to make it perfect.

The skiing championships had already begun. Like a
vast circus, they moved around the world from Europe
to America, even to Japan, skiing different heats in each
mountain area they visited. From each race, the competitors would gain points, and each individual title
would be decided by adding up each racer's five best
scores, the top score possible in each skiing discipline—

slalom, downhill, giant slalom, the 'combined' event, and the new 'super G', which involved the best of downhill skiing together with the swooping, spectacular grace of the giant slalom.

By January, Kate knew that Max was doing well in his races. With the 'circus' coming to Crans Montana, local interest was high and everyone watched the television coverage. The other reps with whom Kate shared the apartment switched the set on as soon as they came in, hoping for more news, and more than once Kate—reluctant but fascinated—saw Max, a scarlet arrow in his skin-tight racing suit, completing yet another fast descent and being greeted at the finish by a crowd of excited friends.

On such occasions, she couldn't help looking for Helga. But the German girl's tawny head never appeared. Did she find it difficult to be supporting a British racer, when her own countrymen were taking part as well? Had she and Max parted, or was she remaining discreetly in the background? Kate knew no one she could ask—and she didn't want to draw attention to her interest in Max, anyway. She kept quiet when the others talked about the championships, and her dread of their arrival in Crans Montana grew daily, until at last the end of January arrived and crowds of skiers, officials, Press and spectators came to fill the two Alpine villages to bursting-point.

'Hello, all alone?' one of the male reps observed one day when he came into the apartment to find Kate alone, trying to read, and succeeding only in thinking about Max and wondering if he might be out there at this very moment, walking down the icy street. 'Aren't you interested in the preliminaries?'

'Oh, yes—I like watching them.' Kate stretched out in her chair and smiled at him. Rob was rather nice, she thought, letting her eyes move over his ruffled brown hair and pleasantly untidy pullover and trousers. 'But I like to be quiet occasionally—on my own. Don't think I'm asking you to go,' she added hastily, realising that her words could be misinterpreted. 'I *was* beginning to feel a bit lonely, to tell you the truth. But there's usually such an uproar in here, the idea of peaceful conversation is something I've rather give up hope of.'

He grinned. 'You're right there. Well. . .it's quiet enough now. Why not have a private discussion of our own? Decide who's *really* going to win. Or—a better idea—why not go out and have a pizza somewhere together? I've got an idea it's Janetta's turn to cook tonight, and I don't really think I can face one of her stews.'

Kate laughed. The apartment contained six reps, each of whom had their own bedroom, but the living-room and kitchen had to be shared and they had decided to take turns in cooking a main meal that could be eaten by all, if required. As it turned out, it was rare that all six ate together; there were frequent evening activities that kept them busy, one or two—like Kate—preferred to eat some of their meals in the hotels where they had guests staying, and occasionally someone would decide to cook their own meal, anyway. But the big bowl of stew or soup, or the pan full of sauce for spaghetti, usually got finished up, one way or another, and nobody minded that they had cooked for six and only fed three or four.

Tonight's cook, Janetta, was famous for stews which seemed to contain almost every ingredient known to man. Sometimes they were a gastronomical miracle; on other occasions, there were so many flavours blended together that the finished meal tasted of nothing at all.

'A pizza sounds lovely,' she said, and they gathered together their thick ski-jackets and gloves, pushed their feet into large, soft moon-boots, and set out.

On the way, Rob chatted freely, telling Kate all about himself. He had had a very ordinary life, he said—his father was a clerk in a solicitor's office and there had never been much money, but he'd done fairly well at school and gone to one of the redbrick universities. He had two sisters, both older than himself and married now, with young children. 'I suppose I was the spoilt baby brother,' he said with a disarming smile, 'but I had a very happy childhood, and we're all still quite close now. Dad will be retiring in a year or so, and then he'll probably devote all his time to his garden, instead of just every evening and all weekend—he ought to have been a professional gardener really, as his own father was, but his parents thought white-collar workers had more status than the men who got their hands dirty.'

'And what does your mother do?' Kate asked, picturing the little town where Rob's parents lived and the quiet way of life they seemed to enjoy. The sort of life she'd never known, with a husband and father coming home from work at the same time each day, and the children going to day-schools and sitting round the tea-table together at five o'clock, teasing each other and competing for the last slice of cake.

'Do? Nothing—she's just Mum,' Rob said with a cheerful grin. 'The sort women's libbers tear their hair out over—but she's happy, cooking and running the house and looking after the neighbours. We've got one or two quite elderly ones, and if it weren't for Mum they'd probably be in homes, but she takes them in a share of the dinner she cooks for Dad and does a bit of shopping for them, and sits with them for an hour or so in the afternoons... And there's the church up the road—she helps with all the jumble sales and coffee mornings, and goes to the women's meetings. Things like that. She always seems to be busy, anyway.' He paused and then added, 'She's one of a dying species, my mum. There won't be any like her soon, when women have all got careers, and then who'll do all the things she finds time for?'

Kate couldn't answer. She had heard so many girls of her own age scorn those who stayed at home, and yet weren't the kind of everyday tasks Rob's mother carried out so cheerfully just as essential to the community as the more high-powered jobs women were encouraged to take up? As Rob said—when there were no women at home, with time to spare, who would look after the elderly people who wanted to stay in their own homes, and who would run the small local charities and keep the spirit of a local community alive?

'I suppose the answer is that everyone should do what they feel is right for them,' she said slowly. 'Go out to work if you like—stay at home if you like. Without having other people criticise and try to run your life for you.'

'And now,' Rob said, pausing outside a warmly lit restaurant, 'you're talking about ideals. People are never going to be that tolerant. We always feel we know what other people ought to be doing, don't we?'

Do we? Kate wondered, and then thought with a stab of guilt about Max—hadn't she criticised *his* way of life?

Hadn't she felt—and said—that he was wrong to strive
so hard for a skiing trophy? Was she herself as guilty as
anyone else of intolerance—of believing herself to know
better than Max how he should live his own life?

And I said *he* was arrogant! she thought in dismay.
She remembered her resolve, that day in Salzburg
airport, to ask him *why* winning was so important to
him.

His reason might have influenced her own attitude
towards him. And she'd thought she loved him—what
kind of love was that? If you loved someone, didn't it
mean you accepted them for what they were—not what
you thought they ought to be? If she'd really loved Max,
shouldn't she have loved him as an ambitious man, a
skier who wanted to win? And why couldn't she do that?

Because I was afraid of getting hurt, she thought. But
getting hurt's a part of life. You can't hide from it
forever. You can't shelter from every storm—sometimes,
you just have to get wet.

'You've gone quiet again,' Rob accused her. 'One day,
Kate, I'm going to ask you what it is that puts that look
on your face. But not now. Tell me what kind of pizza
you want, instead.'

Kate came back to attention and gave him a guilty
smile. It really wasn't fair to come out with Rob for the
evening and then spend her time miles away, her
thoughts with another man.

'There's a long list of them here,' he said, handing her
the menu. 'Me, I go for ordinary cheese and tomato. But
then I'm pretty ordinary all round.'

Kate looked at him. He wasn't fishing for compli-
ments—merely stating what he saw to be a fact. And he
was right, she thought with sudden affection. He *was*

ordinary—there was nothing outstanding about Rob. He had a pleasant face, with a smile that made you feel you could trust him; when he grew older, he would be the kind of man children ran to and neighbours turnd to in times of trouble. He was reasonably intelligent, without being academic or off-puttingly know-all; you could carry on an interesting conversation with him without being afraid he would take the subject out of your range, or above your head. He would never do anything outstanding, but he would always be comfortable to be with.

The sort of man, perhaps, that she'd been looking for—in the days when she *had* looked—to settle down with her in the home she'd dreamed of.

But I'm not looking now, Kate reminded herself. I decided to stay single, didn't I? And, nice though Rob is, the fact remains—I'm not in love with him.

'I'll have the mushroom pizza,' she said, handing the menu back. 'At least, I suppose that's what they mean by *"funghi"*—it never sounds quite so attractive, does it? I always expect all kinds of weirdly shaped objects, but it usually turns out to be ordinary common or garden mushrooms.'

'So,' Rob said when they had been served with drinks and were waiting for their pizzas to arrive, 'how do you like it here in Crans Montana? Nothing like other ski resorts, of course, once the races get going.' He grinned ruefully as a large skier, wearing a thickly padded jacket that turned him into something resembling a circus freak, lurched against him and almost knocked the glass from his hand. 'Did we come out for quiet conversation? But there's something about it—the atmosphere. It's so exciting. And everyone forgets all about their own skiing—well, they haven't come here for that, have they, really? Everyone's come just to watch the races, this fortnight.'

Kate nodded. There was no way she could tell Rob that she must be the only person in Crans Montana who *hadn't* come to watch the races. Or that she would gratefully hide herself away in the apartment for the whole fortnight if she could. She'd even thought wistfully about a dose of flu, but she was seldom ill and didn't seem able to raise even a sniffle.

The thought of meeting Max again threw her into a tumult of emotion. Shame at the way she'd behaved at their last meeting, over the intolerance she'd shown in general, and the arrogance she'd only just discovered in herself, also, the knowledge that she was as deeply in love with him as ever. I'll never get over him while I still keep meeting him, she thought miserably, and made up her mind that next year she would not work as a rep in a ski resort. She would ask Frank to send her to Greece again, or to some other warm holiday area. Even further afield, perhaps—the Caribbean, or maybe India. They'd started tours in China, too—perhaps there'd be a chance for her to——

'You're doing it again!' Rob accused her, and she came to with a start and gave him an apologetic look.

'I'm sorry. I'm not good company at all, I'm afraid. I've got one or two things on my mind and——' Her voice stopped abruptly, and her eyes fixed on someone coming in through the door, taking on a stunned, glassy look that had Rob turning anxiously in his chair.

A small group of racers had just come in, talking and laughing together. The noise in the restaurant lessened as other people recognised them too. They glanced around the big room to find a vacant table, and one of them caught Kate's eye.

He was tall, broad and black-haired. His face was tanned to a deep bronze from a full year spent skiing on high mountains. His eyes glittered like precious stones against the gleaming brown skin—sapphires, overlaid with turquoise glints.

'Max. . .' she breathed, and felt her heart turn over, slowly, and her body turn to shivering ice.

Max Sarsby was perfectly still. His powerful body was poised with all the alert strength of a top athlete, finely tuned to respond with the swiftness of a lightning flash to any situation, yet for the moment, it seemed, frozen where he stood. His eyes met Kate's with a blaze of smouldering fire, and all other sound faded, her surroundings receding as she stared back at him. There was nobody in the room but the two of them; there was no room, only a vast, swinging space in which they orbited helplessly, almost and yet not quite within reach.

And then Max stirred. With the quick, fluid movement of a cat pouncing for the kill, he was across the room and had Kate by the wrist. He jerked her to her feet and she came unprotestingly, her eyes still on that blazing face, her own cheeks white. Still he said nothing; she was dimly aware of the other people again, staring with interest as Max pulled her hard against him and glowered down into her eyes.

'Kate! What's happening?' Rob was on his feet, too, staring anxiously from one to the other. 'Are you all right? Do you want me to——'

'It's all right,' Kate stuttered, finding her voice as Max began to haul her unceremoniously from the room.

'It's all right, Rob. I—I'll explain later. And I'm sorry—
sorry about the pizza, I. . .'

Her last sight, just before Max dragged her through
the door, was of Rob's startled and bewildered face as
he stared after them. And of the waitress, standing close
beside him, with a confused expression on her face as
she held out two steaming pizzas: one cheese and tomato,
and one *funghi*.

CHAPTER ELEVEN

ONCE out in the street, Kate's senses cleared a little. She tried desperately to pull her wrist from Max's grasp, but he simply clamped his fingers all the tighter around her slender arm. The freezing air bit into her bones, and she realised that her jacket had been left behind, in the restaurant. Half sobbing with frustration and cold, she stumbled along in Max's wake, aware of the curious glances and the smiles of passers-by. Where on earth was he taking her?

They came to the wide, brightly lit doorway of one of the village's most expensive hotels, and Max turned abruptly and towed her inside.

'Where are we going? What are you doing? Max, *please*. . .' But her expostulations went unheeded until, having negotiated a lift and a length of softly carpeted corridor, he thrust open a bedroom door and swept her inside.

'There!'

The door was slammed and locked behind him. He released her wrist, and Kate, rubbing it with her other hand, advanced slowly into the room.

'Now,' Max grated, 'perhaps we can get a few things sorted out.'

Kate wheeled round to face him.

'Sorted out? What do you mean? What things? As far as I'm concerned, there's nothing to sort out—nothing! You and I said goodbye a year ago, Max, and I thought it was goodbye forever. I *hoped* it was goodbye forever! Now—let me go. I've got a pizza waiting for me, back in that restaurant, and a rather pleasant companion to go with it.'

'Then I'm afraid they'll both have to go on waiting. I'm not letting you go, Kate, and that's final. I've got a few things to say to you—things you might not like, but you're damned well going to hear them all the same. So just be quiet for a while, if you can—it'll be a new experience for you. And for once in your life, listen. You might be quite surprised by what you——'

'I will *not* be quiet!' she stormed, clenching her fists. 'Neither will I listen. Just who do you think you are, Max Sarsby, dragging me here like this? You virtually kidnapped me, do you realise that? You brought me here by force—there's a law against that and——'

'Go ahead,' he advised, leaning against the door. 'Call the police. What a headline it will make—"Holiday Rep Abducted by Ski Champ". Make all the best gossip columns, I shouldn't wonder.'

Kate glared at him.

'And you'd like that, I suppose. After all, you don't feature too much in the world's headlines, do you?' she said sarcastically. 'And it'll probably be your only chance of getting called a "ski champ".'

Max stared at her and his expression hardened. He stepped forward and gripped her forearms.

'You'll apologise for that,' he said quietly, and for a long moment they met each other's eyes, glances sparring, neither willing to drop first.

'I apologise,' Kate said evenly. 'You might well get another chance.' Max grunted and released her arms, and she continued coolly, 'You've done very well in the races so far, Max. I'm sure you're pleased.'

'Not yet,' he said grimly. 'Not until I've finally won— and got things sorted out with you.'

Kate shook her head. 'I've told you, there's nothing to sort out. Look—what's happened between us? We met—we fought a bit—we made it up. We never even got to be friends, not really. There was always something liable to go wrong. We're better off apart, Max, and that's the truth of it. All right, there's a chemistry between us—an attraction, if you like. But it couldn't ever be anything more than that. We're too different.'

'Are we?' he said. 'I would have thought we were very similar.'

'*Similar*?' Kate gave a short laugh. 'Max, there's nothing at all alike between us two. We want completely different things.'

'Do we?' He moved away from the door and glanced around the room. 'Does this remind you of anything?' he asked, as if changing the subject.

'Remind me of anything?' Kate looked around and remembered another hotel room, in another skiing village, in another country. That was where she had last seen Max Sarsby. And suddenly all the ecstasy and the pain of that evening flooded back over her, and she bent her head as the memory brought hot tears stinging to her eyes.

'Why have you brought me here, Max?' she asked in a low voice. 'I thought you went away from St Joachim because you never wanted to see me again.'

'Yes. I thought that, too.' His voice was harsh, as unlike the velvet tones in which he had spoken that night as the voice of a crow is unlike the fluid sweetness of a blackbird. 'It seems we were both wrong.'

'Wrong?' Kate stared at him. She shivered suddenly and Max came forward quickly, his face concerned.

'Kate—you've got no jacket on, you must be frozen. I didn't realise. . .'

'It's all right.' She stood passively while he found a thick sweater and draped it round her shoulders. 'Max, what is this all about? Why did you bring me here— virtually kidnapping me? I was having supper with a friend—he'll be wondering——'

'A friend?' he cut in sharply. 'Is that all he is?'

'Yes, it is, as it happens,' she retorted, impatience returning abruptly as her numbed brain began to work again. 'But even if it were *not* all, I don't see what business it is of——'

'Mine. No, I don't suppose you do.' Max turned away and passed a hand over his black hair, and Kate, watching him, thought suddenly that he looked tired. Was the racing proving too much for him, after all? 'To tell you the truth, Kate, I can't answer any of your questions. I don't *know* why I brought you here. After all, I've not had much time in which to think it out—I'd no idea you were in Crans Montana until I saw you in that restaurant. And then I—well, I just knew we had to get away together. To talk.' He looked at her, his strong face drawn with emotions she couldn't under-stand. 'Now ask me what we need to talk about.'

Kate looked at him doubtfully. It was almost a year since she had last seen him. Since then, she had finished her season in St Joachim, had her own holiday in Britain, and done a short-term job in Greece. She had met several hundred people in the course of her work, and had liked many of them; she had even made a few friends, mostly among other reps. She had had a few dates with other men, and had even tried—as she'd almost tried this evening—to fall in love with one or two of them.

And there had not been one day when she had not thought of Max, when she had not relived their moments together: the days of skiing, of snow and sunshine and laughter; the moments at Frau Brunner's table, when their eyes had met and spoken more clearly than they seemed able to do with their voices; the morning of the race, when they had dressed as a rabbit and a tiger and skied hand in hand down the long, gentle nursery slope, stopping to kiss at the gate; and the evening when Max had taken her to the hotel room and kissed her, and asked her to give herself to supporting him through this gruelling World Championship.

There had not been one single day in the past year when she had not thought of all that, when she had not longed desperately, fiercely, agonisingly for just one more sight of him, just one more touch.

Had he been thinking of her, too, during those long months?

'But you left me,' she said as if she was thinking aloud. 'When I came home that night—you'd gone. And Frau Brunner said Helga had gone with you.'

'*You* left *me*,' he replied as if correcting her. 'You told me you could never love a man who was as obsessively competitive as I was. You told me I was wasting my abilities. You gave me to understand,' he said in a low voice, 'that you utterly despised me.'

Kate was silent. She looked at Max and listened to the tone of his voice, and she thought, I really hurt him.

Those things I said—they hit him hard. And then she remembered her reflections earlier that evening, while she and Rob had been talking. About tolerance and arrogance, and not trying to run other people's lives for them.

'Max,' she said, moving towards him, 'there's something I want to tell you——'

He stopped her, laying his hands on her shoulders and then touching her lips with one finger. 'There are things I want to tell you, too,' he said. 'We've got a lot of talking to do, Kate, and I don't know what conclusions we'll come to. But I don't know—I'm almost afraid to start.'

'Afraid?' Her eyes were green in the dim glow of the one lamp Max had lit. She looked up into his face.

He sighed. 'This is going to reinforce all those ideals you have about my selfishness,' he said ruefully. 'But these races do matter to me, Kate, and I want to explain why. Meanwhile—tomorrow's race is an important one in the championships. It could almost be decisive. I need rest—rest and security and comfort. With that as a basis, I can go out tomorrow and cope with whatever the course throws at me.' His hands were warm on her shoulders, his thumbs moving gently against her neck. 'Kate—for tonight—could we call a truce? Just practise being friends?' The tension in his fingers throbbed through her body. 'Kate, I need the comfort you can give me,' he said in a low voice. 'I know you don't approve—I know what you think of me. But if you'll just stay. . . Hell, I don't think I can ever explain to you how much I need you to stay tonight!'

It was that final cry for help, which seemed to force its way from his reluctant lips, that decided her. With one swift movement Kate was in his arms, straining her body towards him, pressing him close against her. She felt his strength encompass her, strength that had been slowly increased over months of rigorous training and was now at its peak. How could any man so strong still need help and comfort? She didn't know; nor did she know whether, in the cold light of tomorrow morning, she would regret her decision to stay. But Max had said he needed her, and that, for the moment, was all that mattered.

'I'll stay,' she whispered. 'I'll be with you, Max—as long as you need me.' And she lifted her face to his and reached up to touch his lips with her own.

With a muffled groan he caught her hard against him, and she felt the outline of his body, all bone and sinewy muscle. He had driven himself to the limit, she thought, training for this championship, and wondered yet again whether it could all be worth it, why he did it. But the thought was no sooner in mind than she pushed it firmly out again. Hadn't she vowed not to judge him again— not to question his motives, but to accept his decisions regarding his own life? Max had told her that they would talk—that he would explain why this trophy meant so much to him. But in the light of her new thinking, she wasn't sure she wanted that. Wasn't it a better proof of her love—if he still wanted it—that she didn't ask, that she could give him her heart without needing to know all that was in his?

But did he really want her heart? Even now, she wasn't sure. Somewhere in all this, there was still Helga. Max's vulnerability tonight might be caused solely by her absence. And that might be due to any number of reasons.

Max tore his lips from hers with a reluctance that echoed through her own seeking body. He looked down at her, his smile rueful.

'The first night together for a year, and I can't take advantage of it—or of you!' he said wryly. 'Kate, I'm no company for man nor beast this evening, and certainly not for a woman. The race tomorrow—it's going to take every ounce of energy I have. And you know what that means, don't you?'

Kate smiled. She leaned back in his arms and teased him with her eyes. 'No sex please, we're skiers—is that it?' she said, a laugh in her voice. 'And just who do you think is going to believe that. . .? As it happens, Max, I didn't come here panting to be thrown on to your bed, and I don't at all mind spending a night very chastely here with you.' In fact, she thought, it was something of a relief—making love with Max Sarsby was going to be a new experience, so totally new that she needed time in which to lead up to it. The time an old-fashioned courtship would have provided, enabling them both to get to know each other slowly and thoroughly before taking that final step. But, with the kind of chemistry there was between them, a slow wooing was unlikely ever to happen; the force which brought their bodies together was too immense to be resisted for long, and she knew with a surge of apprehensive excitement that if they stayed together for one night without making love, it would probably be as much as either of them could manage.

Max loosened his arms around her and she moved away from him. The best thing was to keep busy. She glanced at her watch. It was early yet. She remembered the pizza she had left and felt suddenly hungry.

'How about some supper? Could we get some sent up?'

He grinned at her and the tension in the atmosphere relaxed. 'A good idea. I didn't know you had a motherly side, Kate!'

'There's a lot you don't know about me,' she said soberly. 'There's a lot we don't know about each other.' She watched as he lifted the telephone and ordered wine, sandwiches and coffee. 'Max, let me ring my apartment to tell them I'm all right—Rob must be wondering what on earth has happened. And then we'll talk for a while.'

'The whole night, if it helps,' he said, but she shook her head.

'You've got to rest, remember?' She made her call, and by the time she had finished the sandwiches had arrived. Max opened the wine and they sat down on the low sofa to eat.

For a while they sat quietly, both relishing the companionable silence. It was the first time, Kate thought, that they had been together without tension between them, and she wondered just what had caused that tension. The physical attraction that was so undeniable, which they had, nevertheless, both tried to deny? Was it merely physical, or was there something deeper? She believed now that there was, but she still wasn't entirely sure of Max's feelings. It was so easy to make a mistake. And she didn't want whatever happened tonight to create a barrier between them tomorrow.

'Max,' she said at last in a low voice, 'I'm sorry about that night in St Joachim—I'm sorry for walking out on you and for the things I said. They—I believed them then, but I've had time to think and——'

'Ssh.' He put his finger against her lips. 'I don't want

your apologies, Kate. You had every right to think the way you did. I only wish——'

'But I didn't! I didn't have any right to think such things—or to say them. I was making judgements, the sort of judgement nobody has any right to make. You have to live your life the way *you* want to, Max—we all do. For whatever reasons seem to you to be right. And nobody else has any right to say those reasons aren't valid.'

Max smiled. 'You see things so much in black and white, don't you, Kate?' he said. 'Last year, you saw everything I did as wrong. Now it's right—though you don't know why. The truth is somewhere in that fuzzy grey area in between.' He pushed his plate aside and poured a little more wine into Kate's glass. 'I think it's time to talk now, don't you?'

Kate stood up and moved the small table away from the sofa. She stood for a few moments fiddling with the things on it, tidying the plates, stacking them unnecessarily. Now that the moment had come, she was acutely nervous. She wanted to prolong the hiatus, keep this last little space between knowing and not knowing, but at last she was forced to turn and go slowly back to sit beside Max on the soft cushions.

'You told me quite a lot about yourself, Kate,' he said quietly. 'But I feel there's still something you haven't told me—something important, which will explain things I haven't understood. Maybe you'll never be able to tell me—I don't know. But let me tell you about myself. Why I came back to skiing, and why these championships are so important to me. Then perhaps you'll be able to show me your own heart.'

'Max,' Kate said, 'you don't have to tell me anything——'

'But I do.' His deep blue eyes with their disturbing
hint of turquoise smiled into hers. 'I do have to tell you.
Because there's got to be honesty between us, Kate,
whatever comes of this. We may still find there are
differences between us that are too great to be recon-
ciled—but we've got to make that decision on a basis of
complete honesty—don't you agree?'

She could only nod her agreement. 'Whatever comes
of this,' he had said. And, 'We may still find there are
differences.' He wasn't sure—yet. She curled her fingers
into her palms and waited.

'I started skiing when I was a child,' he said. 'I was
lucky, like you—I had parents who loved skiing. My
mother was Austrian and practically grew up on skis,
and we came every year to stay with her family. We
spent Christmas and Easter skiing, and the half-term
weeks as well. At weekends, we went to Scotland—
fortunately we lived near enough to make the journey
feasible, and my parents bought a cottage near the best
slopes. They weren't quite so organised there then, but
you could keep in practice and I was learning all the
time. I wanted nothing else but to be a champion.'

'But you couldn't make a living skiing,' Kate said.
'Surely you must have trained for some profession?'

'Oh, yes, I did that.' He gave her a wry glance. 'I
trained as a doctor. I was always interested in medicine—my father was a doctor, too, and I knew what the
life was like. I intended to make it my career.' His eyes
were grave. 'I still do. But—well, the skiing bug got in
the way.' His mouth twisted a little. 'You were right
about me, Kate—I was out for the glory and the thrill

of skiing to win. I was obsessed. Nothing else mattered to me but winning the next race, the next championship. I gave myself to it completely, without a thought for what it really meant.'

He took a sip of water—he had drunk only one small glass of wine during the meal because of the next day's race. Kate watched him, wondering what was so different about the time he was talking about now, and the present day. Wasn't he still determined to win—still obsessed?

'I spent all my spare time skiing,' he said. 'When I couldn't get abroad, I trained in England, on dry slopes. My training suffered, and eventually it became clear that it had to be one or the other and—well, you know which I chose.'

'And what did your father think of that?'

'He wasn't at all pleased!' Max said with a short laugh. 'Particularly as I was very near the end of my training. He did everything he could to change my mind, persuade me to finish—but I wouldn't listen. Time was going by too quickly; I could be a doctor for the rest of my life, but I couldn't be a champion skier for ever. And not at all if I didn't do it soon!' He stared at his hands, then looked up to meet her eyes. 'Maybe I had to get it out of my system, but there was nothing anyone could do or say to make me see what I was—totally, blindly obsessed.'

Kate said nothing. She could not argue with him, even though she had declared her intention of never 'judging' again. But Max wasn't asking for judgement now; he was stating facts as he saw them.

'Well, then I had my accident. And it was the best thing that ever happened to me.'

Kate's head jerked up in surprise. 'The best thing? But——'

'The very best,' he said firmly. 'It took me out of skiing, forcibly, and back into my other world. The world of medicine.' He was silent then for several minutes, and his hand found Kate's, covering it and squeezing it with a tightness that revealed his emotion. 'It also showed me what I could be doing—ought to be doing.' He turned to her with a suddenness that startled her, and his voice was low and passionate. 'I'd never been into that kind of hospital, Kate. I'd never seen people who were so badly injured that they would never recover, people who were doomed to spend the rest of their lives in wheelchairs, or even worse.' His face was grave. 'I saw young men who'd broken their necks in water-skiing accidents, or on motorbikes—almost totally paralysed, able to use perhaps one finger. I saw small children who would never walk again, older people whose family lives had been completely disrupted by an accident at work, perhaps, or illness. I so nearly became one of them, Kate. I so nearly gave up. My doctors thought I'd never walk again, and for a while I believed them. And then—one day—I realised that I *did* still have movement. I realised that if I kept at it, persevered, I would be able to walk again—and not only walk, but ski. And I made up my mind that I'd do it.' His fingers were almost crushing hers now, but Kate kept still and silent. She could not interrupt the impassioned flow of words. It was clear that Max was telling her things he'd never spoken of before, and there was no way in which she could have stopped him now.

'But I didn't want to ski for myself any more,' he said, and his eyes were burning into hers. 'You've got to believe that, Kate. I still wanted to win—I still wanted the glory—but no longer for myself. I wanted it for *them*.'

'For—them?'

He nodded. 'For all the patients I knew in that hospital. I wanted to do it for them, because they helped me so much. Because even those who knew they would never recover gave me all the encouragement I needed to drag myself back to normality. It wasn't easy, Kate. It meant a lot of hard work and a lot of suffering. There were times when I wanted to give up and lie back and take it easy. But they wouldn't let me. They wanted me to recover—and they wanted me to ski again. They'll all be there now, in front of their TV sets when the races are shown on Sunday, watching and cheering for me. And when I win that trophy—and this time I *am* going to win it—it goes straight back to that hospital, and I'm going to take it to each individual patient to see and to touch, and then it'll stay there on display. To inspire them, if you like—to show them what *can* be done. And—to thank them.'

His words fell into the silence of the room and they both sat very still for a while. Kate's mind moved back over all he had told her, taking it in. She imagined his long days in a hospital bed, first thinking he was doomed to stay there and then, slowly, a fierce determination growing in him to get on to his feet again, to do all the things he'd intended to do—to achieve his greatest ambition. And not, this time, for the self-glorification of which she had accused him, but so that he could inspire other people. As he had inspired her, she remembered, his own courage forcing her out on to the slopes when she'd sworn never to ski again.

The people he spoke of might never be able to recover

as he had, might never walk or run, or even sit up unaided. But his example would be before them like a beacon of hope, shining in the darkness of their world.

'And when you've won?' she asked at last. 'What then? Will you go on skiing?'

'Of course I will! I'll never give up skiing—it's in my blood.' He smiled at her. 'But only for relaxation, Kate. Only for holidays. Because, as soon as I've finished this season, I'm going back to complete my training as a doctor, and when I've qualified I intend to specialise in severely injured people. I hope I'll be able to work at the hospital which helped me so much. Medicine's in my blood too, you see. More deeply than skiing ever was. And I know it now.'

It was late when they finally finished talking—later than it ought to be, Kate thought, for a man who intended winning an important and demanding race the next day. Hesitantly, she suggested that they ought to get some sleep, and Max sighed and agreed.

'You'd better have the bed,' he said, 'and I'll use the couch. Unless—you can go back to the apartment if you like, you know. You don't have to stay with me.'

Kate looked at him. Late as it was, he looked rested and refreshed, a different man from the haunted image he had presented earlier. But there was still a need for comfort there, she could see, a vulnerability that perhaps only she could recognise.

'I said I'd stay. And—we'll share the bed.'

He looked at her with the ghost of a smile.

'I'll borrow a pair of your pyjamas,' Kate said demurely, and that was exactly what she did, changing while Max was in the bathroom. 'I must say, these are rather glamorous. I like black—oh, yes and the red suits you, too,' she added as he came out. 'Now—remember tomorrow's energy requirements!'

Max laughed, the first entirely happy and relaxed sound she had ever heard him make.

'Don't be impertinent, miss!' He drew her down on to the wide bed and they pulled the duvet over themselves. 'Just lie close to me, Kate,' he murmured softly into her ear. 'Just lie close so that I know you're there. . .that's all I want for tonight. . .all I want. . .' He was almost asleep already, she realised, and closed her eyes contentedly. She didn't intend to sleep at all herself—only to savour the closeness of this night. Because even now, things might not work out between Max and herself. And if they didn't—this might be the only night they shared together.

All her instincts told her that it wouldn't be. But— just in case—she intended to stay awake and experience every fleeting minute.

She didn't, of course. In ten minutes they were both fast asleep, breathing gently. For several hours, neither moved; they stayed curled together in each other's arms, very close. As if that was the way it had always been intended that they should.

CHAPTER TWELVE

THE atmosphere in the village the next morning was electric. Everyone was interested in the final race, and intended to find a good vantage-point from which to see it. Max left early to join the other competitors, and make his way up through the lift-system to the top of the course. Kate saw him off, giving him one last hug as he stood, tense and eager, in his skin-tight red racing suit, his crash helmet swinging from one hand. There had been no more time to talk that morning, but she knew that when this race was over they would be able to relax a little and give thought to their future. That it would be together, she had no doubt, and she waited as he stalked away in his stiff boots, confident that nothing, now, could go wrong with their plans.

The sun had already turned the slopes to a dazzling white when Kate had woken that morning. For a few minutes she had lain still, bewildered by her strange surroundings. The window was in the wrong place, she thought dazedly, and why was she in this big bed? And although she could hear the familiar sounds of someone else getting up, running water in the bathroom and whistling cheerfully, the sounds were somehow oddly unfamiliar. None of the other reps in the apartment whistled in quite that way. . .

But she wasn't *in* the apartment! She sat up quickly—and saw Max's ski-suit flung carelessly over a chair.

Max! She was in Max's hotel room. And she'd spent the night in Max's bed.

As Kate looked towards the bathroom door, it opened and Max came into the room, still whistling. He was wearing pyjama trousers and towelling his hair briskly, and when he saw Kate he stopped and gave her a slow smile.

'Kate. Do you know, while I was showering I thought—what if it was all a dream? Will she really be there, in my bed, warm and sleepy and—well, just Kate? I couldn't believe it, somehow—even though I'd only left you a few minutes before.'

There was no sign of vulnerability this morning. The uncertainties of the night had gone; he looked rested, bright and alert. He bent over the bed and kissed Kate on the lips, slowly, lingeringly.

'Did I tell you I love you?' he murmured, and touched her lips again. 'Kate, you don't know what you did for me last night. Just being here. . .I've missed you so much, this past year.'

'Have you?' She held him with her eyes, knowing that now he had said he loved her there was nothing more to worry about. 'And what about Helga? Didn't she make up for my absence?'

'Helga?' He snapped his fingers. 'Kate, there was never anything between Helga and me. I just used her to pace myself—I paid for her time, you know, when she came out skiing with me. It was all fixed up with the chief instructor.' He gave her a shamefaced grin. 'I never mentioned it to you because—well, I suppose I was hoping to make you jealous! Not very laudable, I admit—but we're all human, aren't we? And Helga was happy enough to go along with it, until that last day.'

'Last day?' Kate stared at him. 'But Frau Brunner told me you'd left St Joachim together. And Helga *had* gone—she didn't come back either, not while I was there.'

'No, she went home to Munich. And Frau Brunner was right—we did leave together. I gave her a lift part of the way.' Max sat down on the bed and took Kate in his arms. 'Kate, you never really worried about Helga, did you? Because there really wasn't any need. She was married, you know—she had a husband in Munich. There'd been some kind of row and she'd left him— that's why she was in St Joachim, and why she never did more than work as an instructor. Apparently he rang her up on the night of the race, and they decided to get back together again. *That* was why we left together.' He pulled her close and rocked her in his arms. 'Kate, my darling, what fools we've been. Wasting all this time. . .'

'It was my fault as much as yours.' Kate thought of David. 'There are things I have to tell you, too, Max. But not now. You've got a race to win—remember?'

Wearing one of Max's ski-jackets, Kate followed the crowds to the course. There was still a chance she'd get a place near the finishing line, and that was where she wanted to be, so that she could be there when Max swept triumphantly down the final slope into her waiting arms.

Getting there early enough for a good place meant waiting a long time, but Kate, wrapped up warmly in Max's sweater and jacket, her hands thrust deep into a pair of ski-mittens, didn't notice the cold. She stood close to the fence, hemmed in by other spectators, her eyes already fixed on the towering mountain. Up there,

somewhere, Max was already waiting for the start—
waiting for his turn to thrust away from the starter's hut
and begin his long, swooping descent down the twisting
course.

Like all other downhill races, each skier would do two
runs, the first fifteen of the first run coming down in
reverse order for their second attempt. The event was
now considered, by most international racers, the most
demanding form of competitive skiing, calling for both
tremendous strength and stamina, and exact precision.
The downhill racer needed skill, speed, and aggressive-
ness—yet the impression given to the spectator was of
an effortless grace as the skier flashed down the
mountain.

Kate had watched them preparing the course. She
knew that the special requirements of length, vertical
drop and undulating terrain had all been met. She
became aware of music sounding from the loudspeaker
system, interspersed with brief snatches of announce-
ments and commentary. Not far away were the TV
cameras, ready to record the skiers as they skidded to a
halt at the bottom of the course. Other TV cameras
would be in place at various points on the course, and
there was one right at the top, to catch the competitors
as they began their descent.

It was almost time to start. She found herself shivering, but knew that it was not with cold, simply apprehen-
sion. And suddenly a cold fear shook her—suppose Max
didn't win today? Worse than that—suppose he had
another accident? A crash that would put him straight
back into the hospital bed he had fought so hard to leave
behind? Suppose this time. . .he didn't recover?

She saw Max, confined to a wheelchair for the rest of

his life. Paralysed—unable to use even so much as a finger. . .

'Oh, no. . .' she whispered, her thickly mittened hands against her mouth. 'Please. . .no. . .'

Someone was ringing a cowbell nearby, the tuneless clanging heralding the start of the race. The music stopped, and a voice began to give the order in which the racers would compete.

Max's name was called out tenth.

Tenth! She had to wait for nine skiers to perform before Max came swooping down the mountain towards her. Kate thrust her hands deep into her jacket pockets, and moved her feet restlessly. She craned her neck, staring upwards for the first figure to appear, willing the time to pass quickly. What must Max be feeling like, up there? If only this race were not so important to him!

The excitement around her increased. She could feel the tension in the crowd, a tension which transmitted itself through her own body. The commentator's voice rose, too, as he announced the release of the first racer, and everyone stared upwards, each striving to be first to see the brightly coloured speck of humanity which would quickly—almost impossibly quickly—resolve itself into the shape of a man, crouched in a stance as aggressive as if he were attacking the mountain rather than merely sliding down it. *Merely sliding down it?* Kate found herself laughing almost hysterically at the thought—there was nothing *mere* about any of those taking part in this race today. Like Max, they'd spent months—years—in arduous training, honing their bodies to a peak of fitness that only the world's top athletes ever knew. Like Max, many of them had suffered injuries during the course of their racing—though none of them as bad as his had been—and had overcome them and gone back to the slopes as soon as it had been physically possible. With Max, they shared a common desire—to win—and a common determination which gave them a strength of character and a single-mindedness that was way above average.

Strength and single-mindedness that had frightened Kate; but now, understanding Max's motives for the first time, she saw that they could be used for great good.

And now the first racer was in sight, one of the Austrian team—a brilliant flash of kingfisher-blue coming at an incredible speed down the *piste*. Snow sprayed up from his skis as he sped across the face of the mountain. The spectators who had climbed up through the snow to find view-points beside the course were cheering and ringing their cowbells. The racer swept on, head forward, eyes hidden behind black goggles, and shot under the finishing line.

A good start for the Austrians, Kate thought, watching as the skier pulled off his helmet and shook out his blond hair. He waited anxiously for his time to be announced and looked pleased, grinning cheerfully at his supporters, who were leaning over the fence to slap his back or kiss him as he bent to unclip his skis and lifted them in salute.

The eyes that had been on him a moment before were now trained once again on the glittering hillside. The second skier was about to take off. A Swiss this time. . . Kate stamped her feet and stared up, thinking of Max. Was he conscious of her thoughts, her love, reaching up to him? Did he know that she still didn't really care about the race, only that he should come down the mountain safely? She wondered again about his injuries—could the bones that had been broken, the muscles that had been torn, fail him even now, after all his training? Reason told her that he was as fit as any other athlete here; but still, a voice nagged inside her, he *had* been badly hurt. Could a body ever completely recover from such a trauma?

Couldn't he have helped his friends in the hospital just as much by simply staying there—by finishing his medical training and then doing the work he wanted to do, without having to prove himself first?

You're doing it again, she thought suddenly. Trying to run his life for him, judging him, thinking you know best... A roar from the crowd brought her attention back to the race. The second competitor had fallen somewhere up on the course. Looking up, she could see stewards skiing across to the crumpled body, picking up skis that had come off, bending over the huddled patch of colour.

That could have been Max...

It took some time to bring the injured skier down the mountain. Kate watched miserably, convinced that it was a bad omen. Other skiers would fall and have to be carried away, and Max would be among them. The *piste* was getting harder to ski all the time, every racer making it icier and more dangerous. By the time Max came down...

Stop it! she told herself angrily. Don't you have any faith in him at all? He's a superb skier—you know that. On form, he can win this race easily. And if there were any power in thought—if Max, high on the mountain, could really be affected by the urgency of her own feelings, down here in the valley—then it was positive encouragement he needed, not this fearful depression that seemed intent on seizing her.

Kate gathered herself together. She stared up at the starter's hut, only just within view. Max, she thought, you've got to win. You're *going* to win. And you are not—*not*—going to crash. . .

And then, knowing that it was what Max would have wanted her to do, she gave herself up to the excitement of the race, joining with those around her as they cheered and groaned and swung their black, tuneless cowbells at each competitor. Four had come down; five; six, seven, eight. And then, almost unbearably slowly, the ninth. And at last the commentator announced Max's name and number.

Max Sarsby! The crowd fell silent. Everyone was interested in this man, who had fallen so disastrously and whom they had never expected to see on a ski-slope again. With sudden pleasure, Kate felt the warmth of the crowd reaching out to him. They liked him! she thought with delight. They admired him—they'd always admired him—but now they liked him, too! His reputation for being hard and ruthless, for seizing glory at the expense of all who might stand in his way—it had disappeared. The old Max Sarsby had been left behind; the new one was popular, even loved.

Kate lifted a face that was suddenly glowing. Her body was still tense, but she was no longer afraid. She knew, with quiet certainty, that Max was about to make the most perfect descent of his career, and that nobody else would be able to match it.

The crowd made no sound. They watched the swooping, curving flash of red that seemed to be almost a part of the mountain itself, one with the shining snow. They did no more than sigh as he executed turn after perfect turn, taking jumps like a bird, sweeping with the ease of an angel between the trees. They held their breath as he made the smooth traverse look as gracefully—and deceptively—effortless as a skater's waltz. Only the flurry of snow around him indicated that he made any contact with the *piste* at all; his progress was more allied to flying than to anything that relied on friction.

And then he was approaching the finish. He came under the line in a blaze of triumph, and Kate was almost deafened by the roar that burst from the silent throats to greet his victory—a victory that no one could begrudge him.

She saw him come to a stop and take off his crash helmet. He glanced quickly around as if searching for someone, and, half shyly, Kate lifted her arms and waved.

With a swift skating movement, Max came over to her, ignoring all the hands that reached out to slap him, the smiles and calls of congratulation. The race wasn't won yet, he seemed to be saying; there's the second run yet, and anything can happen.

But as he reached Kate and smiled down at her she knew that he didn't really believe that. This was his day—a magic day. And nothing, now, could stand in the way of his becoming a World Champion.

'More champagne?'

Kate lay back on the sofa and smiled as Max lifted the bottle and tilted it over the two slender flute glasses that stood on the low table. She had never, she thought lazily, known such a blissful sense of relaxation. Never realised what happiness, true happiness, could be.

'You know what?' she said. 'You're quite a man. I wonder why I never realised it from the start.'

'But you did,' Max returned. 'That very first day on the plane—you looked at me and knew I was something special. I saw it in your eyes. Bowled over, you were—admit it.'

Kate laughed. 'The conceit of the man!' she mocked him. 'Shall I tell you what I really *did* think about you that day? That you were just about the most unsociable, rude, arrogant and big-headed male chauvinist pig I'd ever come across in my whole life! And more than that, I——'

'All right, all right!' Max left the champagne and with one swift, springing movement was upon her, forcing her back against the cushions, his hands firmly grasping her wrists so that she was completely helpless. He stared down at her, his eyes glittering, and drew his lips back from his teeth in a snarl that had her cringing.

'Rude, am I?' he whispered. 'Arrogant? Big-headed? *Unsociable*? You're going to regret those words, Kate. . .You're going to wish you'd never said them. . .'

His lips were close to her face as he muttered the last words, and Kate felt a thrill of excitement as they brushed the corner of her mouth. Already trembling with anticipation, she turned her head blindly, seeking his kiss. But Max was not inclined to give it to her yet. He shifted his head slightly, letting his lips move slowly over her cheek, exploring the curling crevices of her ear with his tongue, planting a line of tiny kisses down the edge of her jaw and into the warm, pulsing hollow of her throat.

'Max. . .Max. . .' she whispered pleadingly, and he laughed, somewhere deep in his throat. She felt one hand brush back her flowing hair, leading into a silky caress that brought his fingers down the collar of her satin blouse and into the cleft of her breasts. Gently, he parted the soft fabric, and with sensuous movements began to stroke her breasts, touching the hardening nipples with sensitive fingertips. Kate whimpered a little, stretching in his arms, letting her breasts swell against his tender palms, wanting his gentleness to harden into ferocity, his tenderness to quicken to passion.

But Max, so much in control on the ski-slopes, was equally in control here, in this quiet room. He moved slowly, every touch bringing its own fresh thrill, so that Kate's limbs first tingled and ached, and then grew heavy and languorous in his arms. With fingers that barely brushed her skin, he teased her, bringing her own dormant passion to a flaming wakefulness. He slid her blouse from her shoulders, revealing the firm white flesh beneath, and bent to kiss it; with his mouth, he explored it inch by inch—the rounded smoothness of her shoulders, the soft upper arms, the hollow of her elbow, the fine skin of her inner wrists. He raised her arms and held them above her head so that her breasts lifted towards him, and he let his lips play there, finding the most sensitive spots. And then he covered them with his hands, caressing them with all the reverent care he would have given to a precious piece of porcelain.

Kate lay helpless, almost swooning, under the delicacy of his lovemaking. It was so totally different from what she had expected, this sensitive knowledge of her body. And somehow her own passion, which had cried out for instant gratification, had been simultaneously soothed and increased. She knew now that the rapid lovemaking and climax she had expected would have had none of the mounting joy and promised rapture of Max's almost leisurely exploration. She felt her heart beating, hard and fast, felt the heaviness of her limbs, and then, as Max began to unfasten her skirt, felt his lips at last take hers.

The kiss brought desire surging through her body, had her twisting and writhing against him almost in panic. Love me now, she wanted to cry out, take me, do what you will with me! But Max, as if sensing that her passion was about to reach a height that was no longer tolerable, took his lips from her mouth and held her close, soothing her, although she could feel an answering passion in the hardness of his own body, and knew that he, too, longed for the climax that would bring them the completion they both so desperately needed.

'Ssh, my darling. . .easy, now.' His lips were against her ear, then travelling down the length of her body, between her throbbing breasts, over the softness of her stomach and into the crease of her thighs. . .Kate gasped and twisted again, feeling his mouth seeking her, feeling his fingers bring sensations to her body that could no longer be denied. She lay back, her whole body arched towards him, her fingers tangling in the thick black hair. Oh, soon, she begged silently, soon. Please, Max. . .*please*. . .

Max lifted her knee. He nuzzled his face against it, then slid his mouth down the length of her leg to her instep. With tender lips, he caressed her toes, one by one. And then he left her lying there, helpless and abandoned, while he stood up and rapidly removed his own clothes.

When he stretched himself beside her, their mutual desire could no longer be denied. And then Kate found all the ferocious passion she had imagined, breaking over her body like a storm. She no longer knew nor cared what was happening; she was conscious only of a world that contained only her body and Max's in frenzied contact. They came together in a tangle of limbs, a silky entwining in which their bodies seemed complete for the first time—as if, until now, neither of them had been more than half-finished, two unawakened entities waiting for the moment when life would begin.

Max rose above her at last, his eyes dark and questioning. Faint with desire, Kate could only nod, and then she felt the first, thrusting entry that would make her his for life.

In that last, blinding moment, she was briefly back at the mountain, watching the scarlet figure come towards her down the shimmering slope. She knew again the joy they had shared at the last run which had won him the trophy he'd wanted so much. She saw again, flashing past her, the events that had led to this day, the riotous engagement party they had combined with the celebrations, and their return home to England.

And now they were here, in the flat they had rented while Max completed his medical training. Life wasn't going to be easy for the next few years—he would have to work hard to catch up with his contemporaries and to qualify for the specialist work he wanted so much to do. But the determination that had taken him from a hospital bed to a World Championship would see him through. And Kate's new work as a translator would enable her to stay at his side while she carved her own new career.

She thought once again of the wedding ceremony they had gone through that morning—the ceremony that had made her Kate Sarsby at last. The ceremony they had both decided to wait for before finally giving way to the clamour of their bodies. 'I'm an old-fashioned sort of guy in some ways!' Max had said with a grin, and Kate had laughed and hugged him and loved him for it.

And then all thought left her mind as their two bodies joined in the joyful rhythm that would sustain them throughout their lives, and she knew that nothing else, for the moment, mattered to either of them.

Skiing, championships—none of them were important. Only love. The love of Max and Kate Sarsby.

Take 4 bestselling love stories FREE

Plus get a FREE surprise gift!

PASSPORT TO ROMANCE
SWEEPSTAKES RULES

1. **HOW TO ENTER:** To enter, you must be the age of majority and complete the official entry form, or print your name, address, telephone number and age on a plain piece of paper and mail to: Passport to Romance, P.O. Box 9056, Buffalo, NY 14269-9056. No mechanically reproduced entries accepted.

2. All entries must be received by the CONTEST CLOSING DATE, DECEMBER 31, 1990 TO BE ELIGIBLE.

3. **THE PRIZES:** There will be ten (10) Grand Prizes awarded, each consisting of a choice of a trip for two people from the following list:
   i)   London, England (approximate retail value $5,050 U.S.)
   ii) England, Wales and Scotland (approximate retail value $6,400 U.S.)
   iii) Carribean Cruise (approximate retail value $7,300 U.S.)
   iv) Hawaii (approximate retail value $9,550 U.S.)
   v)   Greek Island Cruise in the Mediterranean (approximate retail value $12,250 U.S.)
   vi) France (approximate retail value $7,300 U.S.)

4. Any winner may choose to receive any trip or a cash alternative prize of $5,000.00 U.S. in lieu of the trip.

5. **GENERAL RULES:** Odds of winning depend on number of entries received.

6. A random draw will be made by Nielsen Promotion Services, an independent judging organization, on January 29, 1991, in Buffalo, NY, at 11:30 a.m. from all eligible entries received on or before the Contest Closing Date.

7. Any Canadian entrants who are selected must correctly answer a time-limited, mathematical skill-testing question in order to win.

8. Full contest rules may be obtained by sending a stamped, self-addressed envelope to: "Passport to Romance Rules Request", P.O. Box 9998, Saint John, New Brunswick, Canada E2L 4N4.

9. Quebec residents may submit any litigation respecting the conduct and awarding of a prize in this contest to the Régie des loteries et courses du Québec.

10. Payment of taxes other than air and hotel taxes is the sole responsibility of the winner.

11. Void where prohibited by law.

COUPON BOOKLET OFFER TERMS

To receive your Free travel-savings coupon booklets, complete the mail-in Offer Certificate on the preceeding page, including the necessary number of proofs-of-purchase, and mail to: Passport to Romance, P.O. Box 9057, Buffalo, NY 14269-9057. The coupon booklets include savings on travel-related products such as car rentals, hotels, cruises, flowers and restaurants. Some restrictions apply. The offer is available in the United States and Canada. Requests must be postmarked by January 25, 1991. Only proofs-of-purchase from specially marked "Passport to Romance" Harlequin® or Silhouette® books will be accepted. The offer certificate must accompany your request and may not be reproduced in any manner. Offer void where prohibited or restricted by law. LIMIT FOUR COUPON BOOKLETS PER NAME, FAMILY, GROUP, ORGANIZATION OR ADDRESS. Please allow up to 8 weeks after receipt of order for shipment. Enter quickly as quantities are limited. Unfulfilled mail-in offer requests will receive free Harlequin® or Silhouette® books (not previously available in retail stores), in quantities equal to the number of proofs-of-purchase required for Levels One to Four, as applicable.

OFFICIAL SWEEPSTAKES
ENTRY FORM

Complete and return this Entry Form immediately—the more Entry Forms you submit, the better your chances of winning!
• Entry Forms must be received by **December 31, 1990**
• A random draw will take place on **January 29, 1991**
• Trip must be taken by **December 31, 1991**

3-HR-3-SW

YES, I want to win a PASSPORT TO ROMANCE vacation for two! I understand the prize includes round-trip air fare, accommodation and a daily spending allowance.

Name_____

Address_____

City_____ State_____ Zip_____

Telephone Number_____ Age_____

Return entries to: **PASSPORT TO ROMANCE**, P.O. Box 9056, Buffalo, NY 14269-9056

COUPON BOOKLET/OFFER CERTIFICATE

Item	LEVEL ONE Booklet 1	LEVEL TWO Booklet 1 & 2	LEVEL THREE Booklet 1, 2 & 3	LEVEL FOUR Booklet 1, 2, 3 & 4
Booklet 1 = $100+	$100+	$100+	$100+	$100+
Booklet 2 = $200+		$200+	$200+	$200+
Booklet 3 = $300+			$300+	$300+
Booklet 4 = $400+	____	____	____	$400+
Approximate Total Value of Savings	$100+	$300+	$600+	$1,000+
# of Proofs of Purchase Required	4	6	12	18
Check One	____	____	____	____

Name_____

Address_____

City_____ State_____ Zip_____

Return Offer Certificates to: **PASSPORT TO ROMANCE**, P.O. Box 9057, Buffalo, NY 14269-9057

Requests must be postmarked by **January 25, 1991**

- ✂ - - - - -

ONE PROOF OF PURCHASE

3-HR-3

To collect your free coupon booklet you must include the necessary number of proofs-of-purchase with a properly completed Offer Certificate

See previous page for details